CATTLE RUSTLER
AND THE
RUNAWAY BRIDE

Brides of Sweet Creek Ranch
Book Four

Wanda Ann Thomas

The Cattle Rustler and the Runaway Bride

Wanda Ann Thomas

Editor: Susan Vaughan
susanvaughan.com

Cover Art::Dar Albert
wickedsmartdesigns.com

Formatting: Seaside Publications
NinaPierce.com

ISBN: 978-1983945113

Chapter One

1892 Cheyenne, Wyoming

A chilly spring breeze buffeted the mud-stained buildings crowding the web of roads, lanes, and railroad tracks converging on the Pacific Union Depot. The jangle of Wyatt Haven's spurs mixed with the rumble of wagon wheels and the shouts of a newspaper boy hawking the latest headlines. But he didn't feel any of the usual enthusiasm that came with a visit to the bustling city of Cheyenne.

Arriving yesterday with three of his brothers to acquire a dozen new Herefords, Wyatt had his own reason for making the four-hundred-mile journey. He halted under the blue-striped canopy outside the ticket office. "Boys, go on ahead without me. I need to check on the train schedule."

"What for?" asked fifteen-year-old, freckle-faced Billy. "We already heard Beau Blackwell's bride-to-be is due on the next train."

Half of Cheyenne had turned out to view the city's

1

wealthiest cattle baron greet Miss Cathryn Cliffton. The young woman in question was said to come from a highfalutin wealthy family who dined regularly with royalty.

Wyatt was equally curious, but he also felt bad for Miss Cliffton. First off because she was going to be Beau Blackwell's wife. And second off because her arrival was being treated like a county-fair sideshow.

Wyatt's decision to leave Wyoming was for the best. He was tempted to sneak away chicken-like to avoid the fight his brothers would put up over the decision. "I won't be returning with you to Sweet Creek," he informed Billy, Garrett, and Ox.

The trio converged on him like a pack of mother hens.

Garrett pushed his brown bangs aside. His new wife kept his hair trimmed so it no longer hung in his eyes, but he had yet to break the habit of swiping his hand across his face. "It wasn't your fault."

Pain lanced through Wyatt and emotion clogged his throat. A seven-year-old boy was dead after attempting to copy one of *his* cockamamie stunts. No amount of talk would make matters right. "Don't go looking gloomy as a preacher presiding over nothing but empty pews. It's time I make a life for myself."

Ox's broad face remained somber. "What about Garrett's Herefords? Aren't you gonna help us get them home?"

Wyatt didn't know when, or if, he'd return to Sweet Creek Ranch, the prettiest spot in the whole wide world. "You don't need my help herding a few cows."

Young Billy's face burned bright red as his hair. "Where will you go?"

Sick over their sadness, Wyatt broke out his monkey impression, making ooh-ooh noises and scratching his arm pits and prancing about pigeon-toed. Passersby laughed, but his bothers didn't relinquish their frowns. "Shoot, boys. It's not like I'm planning to rob banks. I hope to join a circus or a traveling Wild West show as a trick rider. Don't that sound like a hoot? Getting paid to make city folks smile."

Garrett's lips curved upward. "Trick rider? Last I knew you wanted to be a rodeo champion."

Ox finally smiled. "Was that before or after Wy said he wanted to be a chili chef?"

Billy sniffed and scrubbed his sleeve across red-rimmed eyes. "I thought you wanted to be blacksmith."

Ox jabbed Wyatt in the ribs. "You might have to rustle a cow or two so you don't get out of practice."

This was the exact reason Wyatt was leaving the home and the family he loved more than anything. "I'm a numbskull. Getting caught red-handed re-branding Blackwell's prize bull was plain stupid."

Ox shrugged a beefy shoulder. "Blackwell's men stole plenty of our newborn calves this year like they done in years past."

Billy lifted a chin that was as covered in freckles as the rest of his face. "You promised to teach me to rustle cattle."

Wyatt stabbed his finger at Billy. "That's because I'm stupid. I won't have you or anyone else getting killed

3

because of my foolishness."

Garrett shook his head. "You're not stupid or foolish. You keep things fun."

"Tell that to Calvin," Seth said, stalking to a halt in front of them.

Meeting up with Seth was a welcome surprise. Wyatt hoped to patch up the hard feelings with his younger brother.

At nineteen years of age, Seth was putting on muscle fast, and he looked to have grown a couple inches taller during his four-month absence from Sweet Creek Ranch. A wanderer by nature, he never stayed in one place for long. The pure hatred in his eyes remained as intense as went he went away. "Did you get anyone else killed while I was gone?"

The rebuke twisted the knife of guilt eating Wyatt alive. "Everyone back home will be relieved to see you."

"Some of us have real work to do," Seth spit out. "We can't be clowning around all day like you."

"Cut it out, Seth," Garrett said, pushing aside his short bangs.

Billy cast anxious glances at them. "Don't go slugging each other."

A boy who looked to be ten hid in Seth's shadow. His chubby, frightened face was badly bruised. He would be the newest *second-chance boy*. Wyatt's family ran a ranch dedicated to rescuing homeless boys. Wyatt, Garrett, Ox, Billy, and all their other brothers were second-chance boys.

Like this youngster, most of them had arrived battered

and broken. Wyatt had been shot full of bullets when the Havens rescued him. Garrett had been raised in a saloon whorehouse. Wyatt crouched to eye-level, hoping to look less intimidating. "What's your name, son?"

The boy pressed closer to Seth and stuck out a swollen purple lip. "Walter G Whitefield."

Wyatt couldn't help but smile. "That's quite a name for such a little fellow. Should I call you Walt or Walter?"

The boy's over-sized, patched clothes floated on his stocky frame. "My friends call me Wally."

It was good to see Wally still had spirit. Wyatt held out his hand, knowing shaking hands man-to-man filled boys with pride. "Nice to meet you, Wally."

Seth knocked Wyatt's hand away. "Leave him be. Calvin followed you like a worshipful puppy, and it got him killed."

Garrett cast a sympathetic look at Wyatt. "Don't go talking like that."

Ox patted Wyatt's shoulder. "Nobody was at fault."

"It was an accident," Billy added.

Seth bristled like a riled-up grizzly. "Accident, my foot! Wyatt ain't happy unless he's showing off."

Wally's face paled beneath the bruises.

Dying a bit more inside, Wyatt climbed to his feet. Seth had every right to be angry, but the last thing the newest second-chance boy needed was to be surrounded by more violence or hate. "I just told the boys I'm striking out for new pastures. You don't need to be worried about me messing up."

Seth's brows popped, but his eyes quickly clouded.

"You're leaving Sweet Creek Ranch? For good?"

Billy's freckled face puckered. "Mr. Wyatt, you can't go. You promised to help me with my quick draw."

Wally emerged from his shell. "Mr. Seth can learn you how to fire a gun prodigiously fast. He shot my step-dad dead lightning quick."

"Prodigious," Billy repeated, staring wide-eyed at the little boy.

Seth shrugged. "The kid is always spouting fancy words."

Wally's pug face beamed. "A teacher at one of the schools I went to made me sit in a corner and read the dictionary if I talked too much. I made him regret the punishment by entertaining the class with my new splendiferous vocabulary."

Wyatt narrowed his eyes at Seth. "You're supposed to be rescuing abandoned boys, not making them orphans."

"The rotten cuss pulled his gun first," Seth replied defensively.

Wally nodded. "Whiskey made Everett extra stupid and twice as mean as a jail-house dog."

"Doesn't sound like a fair fight," Wyatt observed.

Seth shoved him. "At least, I'm out doing something useful instead of joking and showing off."

Garrett grabbed Seth by the arm. "Quit that!"

Ox grasped hold of Seth's other arm. "Show some respect."

Wyatt took a voluntary step back. "Let him go, boys. Seth has every right to be angry."

Malnourished and defensive when he'd arrived at

6

Sweet Creek Ranch, Seth had never truly settled in. So when he agreed to search for boys needing a second chance, the whole family hoped he'd finally turned a corner. He was so proud when he returned with Calvin. Taking it personal when Calvin died, he went after Wyatt with his fists, then rode away. Four months passed without any word. No one would have been surprised if he disappeared for good. But here he was, plus he'd returned with a second-chance boy. Wyatt wasn't going to mess up the homecoming.

Wyatt hitched his thumb toward the ticket office. "After I purchase my train ticket, I'll meet you boys at the Blushing Rose for a bite of grub."

A whistle blast announced the arrival of the four o'clock train.

Billy's freckled face brightened. "Mr. Wyatt, can we stay and watch them turn the engine around?"

Seth touched Wally's shoulder. "Time to go, kid."

The boy wrinkled his pug nose. "You need to learn to have some fun." But he trudged dutifully after Seth.

"Do you need money for food and shelter?" Wyatt called after them.

Seth strode on without a backward glance. "Go to h—" The train whistle howled again, drowning out the rude reply.

"Fight!" a voice yelled from the opposite direction.

Wyatt glimpsed a knot of cowboys fighting outside the local saloon. But the crowd gathered at the foot of the train platform had eyes only for the first-class passenger car.

A slim young woman with a regal bearing appeared in

the train doorway. Her thick chocolate-brown hair shone like silk. She had to be Beau Blackwell's bride.

Wyatt's feet moved of their own accord.

"Where are you going?" Ox called after him.

Wyatt had to see if she was as beautiful as he suspected. "To say howdy to our new neighbor."

Garrett joined him. "Are you trying to make Blackwell royally angry?"

Hurrying to catch up, Ox spoke between labored breaths. "Wyatt, wait. Blackwell will hang you by the neck if you go flirting with his bride."

"Don't worry boys, I'll behave myself," Wyatt promised.

The sun glistening on his red hair, Billy raced ahead, then turned and jogged backward next to Wyatt. "Ask her to marry you. That would tick off Blackwell good."

Wyatt halted. "Dang. I almost did it again."

His brothers circled him.

"What's wrong?" Billy asked.

Wyatt removed his Stetson and raked his damp hair. This morning's bath had been worth every penny. "I swear I'm done rushing into trouble."

Garrett, Ox, and Billy didn't look convinced.

Wyatt plunked his hat back on his head. "Get me away from here, boys." And he headed in the opposite direction of Beau Blackwell's bride, fighting the temptation to look over his shoulder to capture one more sight of the mysterious woman.

Chapter Two

The steam engine of the train hissed and coughed, belching smoke over the occupants exiting the first-class coach. Miss Cathryn Cliffton of Somerset, England halted on the bottom step.

The cold March breeze carried the bawls of cows and the smell of dung from the nearby stockyard. Closer at hand, a half-dozen cowboys were engaged in a fistfight outside a tawdry establishment having the fanciful name of the Blushing Rose Inn and Saloon. Shoppers bustled in and out the storefronts festooned with sales signs. Three Indians, their faces the bronze shade she had only read about, squatted in the shadows of a white-steepled church, sharing a long pipe and listening to the preaching of a Bible-carrying minister.

The Wild West city of Cheyenne that was to be her new home could not be more different from London. The raw barbarity of the populace and place would cause half of this season's debutantes to faint or go scurrying to their mothers. Kitty relished the adventure. But exploring Cheyenne took second place to her top priority—the comfort and well-being of her ponies.

She grasped the brass railing and, leaning forward, peered at the boxcar near the end of the train. The trip from England to Wyoming had been difficult on Lady Winsome and the rest of her prized polo ponies. She was eager to check on their welfare.

Her brother Milton tapped her shoulder. "Kitten, smile and wave like a good girl to Mr. Blackwell."

A sick wave washed through her. Her husband-to-be stood at center stage on the train platform. Puffy-cheeked with a droopy mustache, the fifty-one-year-old cattle baron had not improved in appearance since his brief visit to her family's country estate.

Standing tall, she forced a smile. "I will attend to the proper civilities and greeting, but then I must see to the unloading of my ponies."

Her brother clutched the lapels of the tweed jacket that once fit him perfectly, but now hung on his emaciated body "They are not your horses yet. Not until after Mr. Blackwell and I sign the contract." Milton gave her a pointed look. "And after you marry."

If their father had not died at an early age, Kitty's marriage might have been more than an expedient business arrangement. "Don't worry, I will do my duty. My ponies are all I need to make me happy."

Milton chuckled. "Is that what you tell yourself?"

She would not be rattled.

Their mother, Mrs. Elaine Cliffton, tapped an ivory-ribbed fan against her palm. "Kitty, move along. You know Milton despises confined spaces."

Did anyone care that Kitty might be the tiniest bit apprehensive at the prospect of marrying an American cattle baron? "Milton and I were discussing my ponies."

Mother wrinkled her nose in disapproval. "Mr. Blackwell does not need you telling him how to care for livestock."

"My ponies are not mere livestock," Kitty protested. "They are the result of years of select breeding."

Milton clucked his tongue. "What will Mr. Blackwell think when he learns he is marrying a horsey girl instead of a proper lady?"

Beau Blackwell stepped forward and tipped his bowler hat in greeting. The four-month engagement had not changed the fact she and Mr. Blackwell were still strangers and that he was close to thirty years her senior.

Kitty told herself it was the smell of Mother's too sweet perfume making her feel sick. She offered Blackwell her hand. Her ponies were worth the sacrifice. She could do this. What other choice did she have? "Mr. Blackwell, it is a pleasure to meet again."

Spongy fingers squeezed her hand. "Miss Cathryn, welcome to Cheyenne. Aren't you looking lovely. Now, if you'll excuse me, I'll leave you and Mrs. Cliffton to the care of Consuela while I attend to your horses. Consuela has instructions to provide you with anything you need." His voice was as brisk as his manner. "Mr. Cliffton, would you care to take a drink at my club while your sister and mother recover from their journey?"

Milton withdrew a gold-trimmed, blue-enamel snuffbox from a hidden silk-lined breast pocket. "Ah yes, the famous Longhorn Club."

Kitty wrapped her arms around her waist to keep from snatching the gaudy snuffbox and flinging away the small valuable at the center of a year's worth of deceit, anguish, and humiliation. She forced her attention to Beau Blackwell. "I don't need to rest. I will join you in overseeing the care of my ponies."

"Kitten, your unwavering concern for my property is touching," Milton said drolly.

She should be used to her brother's hateful teasing by now. "Your profits will suffer if one of the ponies snaps a leg or if an illness goes undiagnosed."

Milton clicked open the snuffbox and extracted a pinch of the yellowish-brown powder. "Then by all means, go fuss over my ponies." Dabbing the powder to a pink-veined nostril, he sniffed deeply.

Beau Blackwell stared at her and then Milton. But at least the man was actually looking at her instead of through her. "My men are perfectly capable of caring for a few polo ponies."

Milton's half-lidded eyes exploded with dangerous euphoria. "Good luck convincing Kitty to desert her ponies. Now if you will excuse me, I'm going to snoop around the Blushing Rose and determine if there are any interesting card games afoot."

Mother beat the air with the yellow fan. "Milton, dear. I know the trip was difficult, being cooped up in the train, and the noise and crowding and horrid food. But do you need to rush off so soon?"

Milton's gaze didn't waver from the saloon. "I do,

Mother. Indeed, I do."

Kitty heard a familiar whinny. Her prized pony, Lady Winsome, pranced in the doorway of a cattle car at the rear of the train. She was resisting the handler cussing at her and yanking on the lead rope. "Who gave that man permission to move my ponies?"

Blackwell flapped his hand in a dismissive manner at the commotion. "Don't fret, my foreman Amos Little will tame that filly."

Kitty pushed past the annoying man. "I am a woman, Mr. Blackwell, not a nitwit."

"Where are you going?" Mother called. "You have to help me talk sense to your brother."

Kitty shoved her way through the hive of activity surrounding the train cars. She had long since acknowledged Milton's dissolute lifestyle as a lost cause. Just as she had resigned herself to explaining to Americans why her polo ponies were not the short and stubby breed of horses they were familiar with. Polo ponies were in fact similar in size and appearance to thoroughbred race horses. And just as valuable. Clearly the ranch foreman mishandling Lady Winsome needed a lesson in the proper care of champion polo ponies.

A whistle shrieked, and steam hissed from a locomotive entering the train station on the maze of tracks constituting the railroad hub. Lady Winsome reared wild-eyed at the new commotion. The foreman yanked hard on the lead rope and cussed louder, adding to the pony's terror.

Kitty raced faster toward the loading ramp. "Stop! You'll hurt her."

Blackwell caught up with her just as she reached the rail car. He captured her arm, jerking her to a stop. "You've exerted yourself enough for one day."

She pulled free. She had not even begun to exert herself. "Winnie, calm down, girl."

"Stay put," Blackwell ordered.

"Here, boss." A dust-covered cowboy handed over a whip.

Blackwell coiled the devilish length of leather and climbed the ramp.

Heart speeding, Kitty followed. "Don't you dare whip my pony."

Ignoring her, Blackwell grabbed the lead rope from the foreman. Winnie reared, slashing a hoof across his forehead, and knocking his bowler hat off his head.

"Cussed horse!" Blackwell touched his hand to a trickle of blood, then lashed the ramp with the whip.

Kitty grabbed his elbow. "Stop that!"

Winnie screeched and charged forward. Breaking free, the pony ran over the foreman in her haste to flee.

Leaving Blackwell and the others to care for the downed man, Kitty chased after her pony. People yelped and scattered. A barking dog raced after Winnie. A fruit-vendor chucked an orange to save his make-shift stand from the stampeding animal, causing Winnie to veer toward a junk-lined alley.

Kitty's throat closed. She pictured all forms of horrific injuries if the dog cornered her poor frightened pony.

Then a broad-shouldered cowboy appeared out of nowhere, twirling a lasso. The rope arced through the air and encircled Winnie's head. Clad in a fringed buckskin jacket, the cowboy dug his boots into the ground. In an elegant ballet between horse and man, the cowboy soon had Winnie trotting around him in a circle.

At the sound of distant whistling, the dog ceased barking and trotted away.

Kitty raced to Lady Winsome and the cowboy, who smiled at her. "Thank you. Thank you. Thank you."

Baby-blue eyes sparkled in a boyishly handsome face. "You're right welcome, ma'am."

Winnie slowed, circling closer as the cowboy carefully reeled in the rope. Kitty approved of his competent yet gentle technique. "She trusts you."

"That proves she ain't got no sense," the cowboy answered, with a smile as wide as the outdoors. "Howdy. My name is Wyatt Haven."

She captured the pony's leather halter and stroked her chestnut cheek. American men came across as larger than life, but this cowboy had a double portion of magnetism. "And I am Miss Cathryn Cliffton."

Some of the light went out of his eyes. "You must be Beau Blackwell's bride."

Admitting the truth hadn't caused her any shyness before now. "You are acquainted with Mr. Blackwell?"

He offered her a chagrined smile. "We ain't exactly on speaking terms."

Beau Blackwell strode up to them and glared at Wyatt. "Darling, you shouldn't be keeping company with this outlaw."

Winnie's nostrils flared, and she shifted away from

Blackwell. Kitty held tighter to the halter. "For heaven's sake, put that whip away and thank Mr. Haven for safely capturing a champion polo pony."

Blackwell hooked the whip to his belt. "I'll eat my hat before I thank this thieving cattle rustler for anything."

"I guess that means I won't be getting an invite to the wedding?" Haven said, his voice casual, but his stance had turned guarded.

Blackwell retrieved a red handkerchief from his back pocket and dabbed at the blood streaking his forehead. "What are you doing in Cheyenne?"

Haven removed his blindingly white cowboy hat and raked his fingers through thick blond waves. "I'm not here to dance a jig at your wedding."

"Everything is a joke to you." Blackwell crammed the blood-stained handkerchief into his back pocket. "If I catch you stealing more of my calves, you won't laugh when you're standing before a judge and jury."

Kitty could not be more flabbergasted. Mr. Haven, a cattle rustler? On the trip from England to America, Milton had regaled her and Mother with tales of the outlaw West, of gunfights and Indian attacks and train robbers. Haven could not possibly be an outlaw. Six foot tall, with bull-like shoulders and neck and a chiseled jaw, he would more readily be mistaken for a Greek god than a cattle rustler.

He grinned. "Good luck finding a jury that will convict me."

"I can always hope you will die in a shootout with the posse," Blackwell said.

The other man's smile slipped. "Amos Little would like

16

nothing better than to shoot me and my brothers full of holes."

A chill went down Kitty's spine. The bad blood between the pair appeared to stem from a longstanding feud. She secured Winnie's halter with both hands. "Lady Winsome has had enough excitement for one day."

"Come along, darling," Blackwell said. "I need to give instructions on dividing the horses as they are unloaded."

She tugged free. "Stop calling me darling. And what sort of instructions?"

"There's no need to fret," he said, as though chastening a distraught two-year-old.

"I am not fretting. And I will see to the care of my ponies," she shot back, suspecting she sounded exactly like a child on the verge of a temper tantrum.

The cowboy coiled the lasso into loose loops. "Ma'am, can I offer you more help before going back about my own business?"

"Vamoose, Wyatt," Blackwell said between gritted teeth. "You've done enough harm for one day."

Regret welled at the need to send this kind cowboy on his way. Which was supremely ridiculous. "Please accept my gratitude and best wishes, Mr. Haven."

"I hate to see you looking so sad," he said in a low voice as Blackwell moved to examine Winnie's hind quarters.

She glanced at her fiancé, with his cold eyes and slouching mustache, then back at the kind, beautiful cowboy. "I have my ponies. They are all I need to make me happy."

Haven stared at her for a long moment as if trying to

see into her soul. "Are you sure, ma'am?"

His genuine concern made her want to weep. "I will be fine." What other choice did she have?

Blackwell shouldered her aside. His face was red with anger. "Miss Cathryn's happiness is none of your business."

Haven narrowed his eyes at Blackwell. "You know nothing about making anyone happy but yourself." Sliding his hat back on his head, he acknowledged her with a nod and a wink. "If you get an itch to be a runaway bride, Miss Cathryn, please call on me for help. I promise you Beau Blackwell won't find our trail."

He strode away without giving her time to reply to the incredible offer. Was he jesting? Or flirting? Or trying to antagonize Blackwell? Kitty worked at gathering her composure. "What an interesting man."

"Wyatt Haven is an insufferable fool," Blackwell growled, gripping her elbow. "My men will drag his sorry hide through the city behind a horse if he dares to bother you again."

Breaking free of his grasp and securing a hold on Winnie's halter, she coaxed the skittish horse toward the train, having all she could do to not to look over her shoulder in the direction the cowboy had gone. "He wasn't bothering me. He rescued Lady Winsome."

It was best to put Wyatt Haven and his outlandish suggestion out of her mind. Running away with an outlaw cowboy was the last thing she would ever do.

Chapter Three

Moments later, Kitty spoke in soothing tones to Lady Winsome as they wove their way through the chaos of the railway yard. "A pail of oats, a drink of clean, cold water, and a bed of fresh straw will help settle you."

She glanced up at the high red-brick clock tower presiding over the train station. Was it only quarter past four? Hours to go until bedtime and escape.

A meaty hand seized her arm. Blackwell's mustache scratched her ear. "If you want to have a happy marriage, don't contradict me in public. Do I make myself clear?"

Lady Winsome pranced nervously. Kitty tightened her grip on the halter. It was clear her husband-to-be was an obnoxious bore and safe to assume contradicting him in private wasn't likely to be welcomed either. "I will not remain quiet if my ponies are being mistreated."

"You and your filly need a firm hand," Blackwell said.

Winnie flattened her ears and swung her rear around. Kitty leaned into the pony's hind quarter to prevent her from getting within kicking distance of Blackwell. "The month-long journey has been difficult on my ponies. Once they reach their new home they will settle down."

Despite the rocky start, she had to believe the necessary move to America would ultimately work out for the best. Her lifelong friend Henrietta Rochester was happy with her American husband and the polo pony ranch they'd established in the shadow of the Bighorn Mountains.

Her husband-to-be tipped his hat at an open carriage drawn by an impressive white gelding. The family's elegant attire suggested they were attending a garden party or some such festive occasion. He plunked the bowler hat back on his head. "You have made enough of a spectacle of yourself for one day. And your mother looks apoplectic. Consuela will assist with your luggage and drawing baths. I want you looking pretty as a picture tomorrow for the wedding."

Her brother was nowhere to be seen. Kitty inspected her wrinkled navy-blue travel dress. Cheyenne's social code had to pale compared to London's rigid standards. Then again, the niceties expected of a cattle baron's wife couldn't be ignored. "How long before we leave for the north? I'm eager to see my wedding gift." Her reunion with Henrietta and the promise of her own polo pony ranch were twin rewards she'd been anticipating for months. And far preferable than dwelling on her coming marriage.

Blackwell stroked his droopy mustache. "I wasn't able to acquire the land I had in mind for your wedding present. But the ponies should be comfortable enough at my Double B Longhorn Ranch until I secure a suitable property."

His dark look told her there was far more to the story,

but now was not the time to pry.

"As long as my ponies have adequate stable boxes and pastures, I will be satisfied." When the engagement was finalized, she had informed him the proposed wedding gift was too generous. But from the first moment they'd been introduced it was evident Blackwell was a prideful showman.

Lady Winsome neighed a greeting to her stablemates as they approached the train. The Double B Ranch foreman was supervising the men busy offloading her ponies.

Kitty gritted her teeth. "What is your foreman's name again?"

"Amos Little."

She led Winnie through the swarm of men inspecting her ponies. She had been present for the birth of all six ponies. Selling off the rest of her stock had been as difficult as the days surrounding her father's death and burial.

Amos Little pointed to a sturdy yearling named Duchess Lovey. "Cavalry." He hitched his thumb over his shoulder as the next pony was led down the ramp. "Sport."

She stumbled on a wagon wheel rut. "Cavalry?"

Blackwell caught her and dragged her against his side. "You and your ponies are an investment. The biggest and strongest horses will be bred for British and American cavalry units. You're free to raise one or two for sport."

She struggled in vain against his hold. "That's not the agreement we made."

A grim chuckle was his answer. "Your brother was

21

desperate to see you well married."

"Cathryn," her mother scolded, yellow fan swishing double-time. "Stop being coy. It is perfectly acceptable for Mr. Blackwell to hold your hand and give you a peck on the cheek."

Why must she pay for Milton's sins? Kitty asked the heavens. She exhaled a harsh breath. "Nothing has been decided yet."

Amos stalked over. "Boss?"

Winnie stretched her neck and nipped Little's ear.

He yelped and staggered backward with his hand clapped to his ear.

Kitty grasped Winnie's halter. "Easy, girl. It is not Mr. Little's fault he has an irritating voice."

Little snatched up a whip and shook it at Lady Winsome. "Bite me again, and it's off to the glue factory with you."

Winnie quivered and pranced. If she reared, Kitty would lose hold of the halter. "Put down that whip!"

"You heard the lady," Blackwell snapped.

Little tossed the whip aside. "I told you these polo ponies were going to be a pain in the backside."

"If I want your business advice, I'll ask for it," his boss said.

The audience of cowboys ranged about the loading ramp laughed.

Kitty stroked Lady Winsome's neck. "Mr. Little, stay away from my ponies and we will get along fine."

"She told you," a cowboy called out.

Little's face pinched. "Stop gawking and get these

horses to the stockyard."

Kitty coaxed Winnie forward. "Mr. Blackwell, would you be so kind as to show me the way to the holding pens? The ponies will move along smartly behind Lady Winsome."

"My men follow my orders, not yours," Blackwell murmured, joining her.

"I would not dream of interfering." She had not crossed an ocean and a half a continent only to give up control of her horses. The sooner her husband-to-be and Amos Little accepted this the better off they'd all be.

<hr />

Two hours after rescuing Lady Winsome, Wyatt stood beside a makeshift stable box admiring the chestnut filly. He breathed in deep, enjoying the homey smells of hay and horse. Cattle bawled in the nearby stockyard, but all was quiet in the coolness of the barn. A soft muzzle swept over his palm, inspecting the gift of bright orange baby carrots. Nibbling lips plucked up the treat.

He stroked the horse's graceful neck. "I bet you don't feel a bit sorry that I have to join a circus. Do you think elephant and lion dung smell much different from horse or cow dung?"

A musical laugh echoed through the barn. Not stomping music played on fiddles and banjos, but that of gentle violins and happy flutes. Miss Cathryn Cliffton strolled toward him, chaperoned by Consuela. "What a nice surprise to find you here, Mr. Haven. I must know what has you musing over the odor of elephant and lion manure."

He'd come to the stable guessing and hoping she'd be unable to resist checking on her horses. She'd exchanged her travel gown for a form-fitting brown velvet outfit. She sure was a one pretty filly. "I'm on my way to join the circus."

Her smile lit up the barn. "Truly?"

Wyatt shrugged. "Afraid so."

Consuela looked like she'd swallowed a prickly pear. "Mr. Blackwell wouldn't approve of your speaking to a cattle rustler."

Miss Cathryn joined Wyatt and patted her pony. "A cattle rustler and a circus performer. How exciting."

Lady Winsome nickered contentedly.

He grinned. "That's a right kindly way to say you're mortified by my choice of employment."

She was trying not to smile. "Are all cowboys as friendly as you?"

"You mean crazy?"

"Joining the circus sounds lovely."

"You wouldn't say that if you ever visited Sweet Creek Ranch." The sturdy ranch house tucked in the majestic shadows of the Bighorn Mountains that had been his home for sixteen years was his idea of heaven.

Consuela shifted uneasily. "Miss Cathryn, your mother instructed you not to be gone long."

Miss Cathryn moved to the next horse box. "Lord Braveheart, do you approve of your temporary home?"

The dappled gray horse sniffed at her white blouse.

Miss Cathryn smiled affectionately, rubbed his ears, and rested her cheek on his searching snout. "I am sure Lady Winsome and Lord Braveheart will be much happier when we reach our destination."

Beau Blackwell's Double B Ranch was one of the largest cattle outfits in the state. Why did he hate the idea of her taking up residence there? "We heard Blackwell was promising to give his bride-to-be a polo pony ranch."

Her eyes clouded. "Will my ponies be pleased with the Double B?"

He didn't like seeing her looking anxious and scared. "I don't know nothing about England, but Wyoming high country feels like living at the edge of the world. Your nearest neighbor is ten to fifteen miles away. Winters can leave you snowbound for four or five months. There's no ballrooms or electric lights or any modern conveniences to speak of, but if I was a horse, I'd think I was in horse paradise. There's green pastures that go on for miles and miles. Sparkling clean mountain streams to drink from. Room to run and kick up your heels."

She rewarded him with her beautiful laugh. "I am glad to know I am not the only person whose mind works like a horse."

"My brothers would say I have a mind like a mule rather than a horse."

Her enticing lips curved. "I have been accused of being a stubborn mule more than once, especially by my father" Her voice deepened to a man-like pitch. "*Don't kick up, Kitty-Girl.*"

Consuela rolled her eyes and muttered in Spanish.

A deep sense of loneliness filled him, wondering when or if he'd reunite with his family and Sweet Creek Ranch. "Tell me about your home."

Consuela stepped between them. "Mr. Haven, if I was you, I would leave now and stay far away from Mr. Blackwell's property."

The warning was not lost on Wyatt. His decision to get another peek at Miss Cathryn was selfish and stupid. Chatting like this was the social hour at a church picnic wasn't doing either of them any favors. He tipped his hat at Consuela. "My mother taught me it's best not to argue with a wise woman."

Miss Cathryn cast a hopeful look at Consuela. "A few more moments cannot hurt."

The servant's chin firmed. "We won't have to mention this to anyone if we hurry back."

Shoulders falling, Miss Cathryn walked a few steps, then turned back. "Your runaway bride suggestion was quite lovely."

Lovely? The words hit harder than a kick from a bull. "I was in the wrong. I shouldn't have said that."

"Do not fear. I will do my duty," Miss Cathryn said in parting.

Was that grief he saw in her beautiful eyes?

Sacrificing happiness for the good of others was one bond they shared. He knew beyond a doubt Blackwell wouldn't cherish her or begin to make her happy. Just like he knew he would never stop missing his home and family.

He drew a small burlap sack from his pocket and dumped the contents in his hand. He thumbed the cameo-sized picture of his real folks, pioneers who had died on the Oregon Trail. The silver bullet that was a gift from the cattle rustler Red Calder. And marbles—red, blue, green, yellow—four of the marbles Calvin had cherished.

Sadness gave way to determination. For once in his life, he would act responsibly.

Chapter Four

Wyatt tapped his foot to the tinkle of piano music and nursed a second glass of root beer. Pungent cigar smoke clouded the confines of the Blushing Rose Inn and Saloon. A famed lady cardsharp called the Jewel of Texas presided over a high-stakes poker game.

Jewel was too racy for his likes. But his run-in two hours earlier with Beau Blackwell's bride still had him considering the charms of a horse-loving gal with an English accent.

His brothers were proving dull companions.

Ox rested his chin on his enormous fists, mooning over a plump saloon-hall dance girl at a nearby table flirting with four cowboys flush with cash from a cattle drive. Billy moaned like sick basset hound thanks to challenging Wyatt to a chili pepper eating contest. Garrett wasn't much of a talker, but offered the occasional comment regarding the Hereford bull and dozen cows he'd purchased.

Wyatt slugged back the root beer. It was stupid of him not to wait until tomorrow to tell the boys about his plans join a circus or Wild West show. The traveling life must have advantages other than making folks smile. But at least his crazy stunts would put only his own neck at risk.

He wiped away the remains of the suds beard and glanced at the saloon door again, hoping Seth would wander in. After checking around, he'd learned Seth and Wally were bunking down at the stable around the corner. Wyatt rubbed his chest, but the deep ache refused to go away. He hated the notion of leaving his home and family behind without trying one more time to mend fences with Seth.

Exhaling heavily, he hoisted his empty glass to catch the eye of the bartender. Yep, it was a three-root-beer kind of night.

A card player losing to the Jewel cursed loudly, tossed in his cards, and stormed out of the saloon.

The buxom cardsharp scooped up the man's coins, then smiled prettily for the room. "Who's feeling lucky?" She winked at the man sitting across the table. "But I must warn you, Mr. Cliffton is a cagey player."

Wyatt grasped the fresh mug of root beer handed to him without taking his eyes off Cliffton. Thin and pale, the man bore little resemblance to his sister. Wyatt hoped Miss Cathryn was surviving her first night at Blackwell's mansion in good spirits. Putting aside the fact she was enduring the man's less-than-pleasant company, the experience had to be difficult.

A strange home. In a strange country. Marrying a stranger.

Come to think on it, why was her brother here, gambling, instead of standing by his sister?

Wyatt plunked the mug on the table, scraped back his chair, and stood. "Luck is my middle name," he called, accepting Jewel's invitation.

A wave of laughter went around the hall.

The Jewel of Texas raised an elegant brow. "Do you have a first and last name, cowboy?"

"You know better than to mess with a cardsharp," Garrett whispered.

Wyatt wasn't a practiced gambler or card player, but a hand or two of poker would allow him a closer look at Cliffton, and give him the opportunity to suggest the callous man return to his sister's side. "Howdy, ma'am. My name is Wyatt Haven."

She eyed him cautiously. "You wouldn't be related to Levi and Ace Haven?"

Wyatt's brothers had regaled the family with tales of their numerous run-ins with the Jewel of Texas. "Do you still own the silver spurs and belt buckle Ace forfeited to you?"

Jewel's smile was forced. "Why, yes I do."

Ox grabbed Wyatt's elbow. "If Ace can't win against the Jewel of Texas, what chance do you stand?"

No one had ever accused Wyatt of being cautious. "Don't waste your worry on me. I'm a big boy."

Garrett stared back doubtful. "Well, if you lose all your money, you won't be able to buy a train ticket."

"Don't say we didn't warn you," Ox grumbled, letting go of Wyatt's arm.

Billy still clutched his gut. "Mr. Wyatt ain't afraid of no lady gambler. Ain't that right?"

Wyatt pushed his root beer toward Billy. "Try this for your stomach."

Billy nodded, admiration beaming in his eyes. "It's gonna be fun watching you outwit the Jewel of Texas."

That put a hitch in Wyatt's giddy-up. Why was it the more he messed up, the more the second-chance boys adored him? He ought to call it a night and tell the boys it was time to head off to bed.

Cliffton wore a bored expression. "My good man, are you going to stand there like a simpleton or are you going to join us?" He retrieved a gold snuffbox from a pocket inside his jacket.

The man's attitude stank. If he talked like that to the wrong cowboy, he might have a few bullet holes decorating his pretty coat. Where would that leave Miss Cathryn? It was clear her brother wasn't concerned with her best interests. Of course, if become necessary to escort Cliffton to Blackwell's mansion, Wyatt just might catch another glimpse of the bride.

Whoa doggie, wouldn't that be worth a little trouble?

"Garrett, make sure Ox and Billy behave themselves." Wyatt strolled away. "Don't stay up late on my account."

An hour later, a good bit of Wyatt's coin had gone into Cliffton's purse. And it was fair to say, he'd never made the acquaintance of a bigger bore or snob than Mr. Milton Cliffton.

The Jewel of Texas was on a losing streak as well, but her charming smile showed no sign of cracking. She stroked the lucky gold coin that was said to come from her first jackpot. "Mr. Cliffton, would you care for a stronger drink than tea?"

He fiddled with the gaudy snuffbox sitting beside his neatly stacked coins. "I'm tempted to switch to something stronger, as your American tea taste like goat p—"

"Watch your language around the lady," Wyatt warned, gathering up the slippery cards and shuffling the deck.

Cliffton looked at him like he was a bug to be squashed under heel. "I wasn't aware there were any *ladies* present."

Jewel stared at him over the glass of amber liquid poised beneath her rosy lips. "I won't be insulted at my own table. Do I make myself clear, Mr. Cliffton?"

The obnoxious man smirked. "Perfectly, *madam*. Perfectly."

Rumor had it the Jewel of Texas kept a loaded pistol close at hand to deal with trouble. Cliffton wouldn't know that, or he would have thought better of suggesting Jewel was a *lady of the evening*.

Wyatt employed a fancy shuffling trick, sending the cards flying in all directions. "Sorry about my butterfingers." He bent and picked the cards off the floor.

Jewel gathered up the cards scattered around the hem of her silk skirt. "I see Ace has been influencing you." Her tone was amused.

"Only for good," Wyatt answered. Straightening, he spied Cliffton trapping Jewel's lucky gold coin beneath the snuff box. He promptly deposited both into his breast pocket.

Did the fool have a death wish?

Jewel leveled a palm-sized Derringer at Cliffton. "Wyatt, fetch back my coin before I put a large hole in this man."

Cliffton sprang to his feet. "I must be off."

Wyatt leaped up, shoved the Derringer aside, and grabbed the man's lapel. "What we have here is a simple misunderstanding." He didn't know what the punishment for thievery was in England, but in these parts people died for offenses large and small. He glared down at Cliffton. "You put Miss Jewel's coin in your pocket by accident. Ain't that right?"

The more sensible saloon patrons quietly slipped away. The remaining onlookers crowded closer and buzzed with anticipation. Garrett, Ox, and Billy shoved their way to the front, hands close to their guns.

"Do you need our help, Wy?" Garrett's stance was anything but casual.

Wyatt pulled Cliffton closer. "We can do this easy like, or hard like."

Eyes beady as a frightened chipmunk, Cliffton slapped at Wyatt's hand. "What is the meaning of this?"

For a dollar and change, Wyatt would hold the man by the ankles and give him a good shake. "Empty your pockets, or I'll do it for you."

Cliffton shot a disgruntled look at Jewel. "Are you questioning my honor?"

Jewel heaved an exasperated breath. "I've met more honest politicians."

Giggles from the saloon girls mixed with male laughter.

Jewel tucked the pistol into her waistband. "Give back the coin and we'll forget about it, and you—" The color drained from her face.

Accompanied by two deputies, Sheriff Deacon Judd muscled his way past the saloon patrons with his gun drawn. "Jewel, did you forget our little talk?"

A smothering blanket of tension fell over the hall.

Jewel lifted a hand to her neck. "Wyatt, please release Mr. Cliffton. You were just having a bit of fun with the gentleman. Isn't that so?"

Wyatt was close enough to see she was trembling, but he couldn't be sure if it was out of fear or anger. He released the other man's lapel and smoothed the wrinkled coat, his fingertips bumping over the outline of the coin. "We were having a friendly discussion about gold coins."

"You win today, Mr. Cliffton," Jewel said hastily.

He chuckled and tidied a tall stack of bills. "I like you Americans. Terribly good sports you are."

Wyatt rubbed his fist, itching to pound Cliffton into the ground. But that wouldn't help Miss Jewel any.

Cliffton captured Jewel's hand and pressed the wad of bills into her palm. "Adieu, my dear. I am off to find more diversion." And he strolled away humming a cheery tune.

Miss Jewel glanced between the fat pile of cash and the sheriff. "Deacon, if you feel need to harass someone, go after Mr. Cliffton. He is certifiably loco."

The sheriff held out his callused hand. "Give me the pistol, darling, unless you'd like me to come take it from you."

Dangling the Derringer by the grip and holding her head high, the Jewel of Texas dropped the gun into his hand and swept to the grand staircase leading to the second-floor guest rooms.

The sheriff chuckled. "Yes, siree, I'm gonna get me some of that sweet—"

"Miss Jewel ain't kidding," Wyatt said, cutting off the crude remark. "Cliffton is as loony as a rabid fox and crooked as the day is long."

Hard eyes raked Wyatt. "Mind your manners while you're in my town. Beau Blackwell warned me about you and your cattle thieving ways. I promise, if any livestock goes missing, I'll track you down and string you up by the neck so fast you will be roasting in hell before the devil knows you're there."

Wyatt didn't like this Deacon Judd fellow one little bit. But he didn't want to rile matters and risk allowing Cliffton to escape. "You won't get no trouble out of me."

Garrett, Ox, and Billy pressed closer.

Wyatt gave them a warning look. "It's time we get going, boys." And he strode outside. The cold wind slapped his face, as he glanced to the right and spied Cliffton enter the Longhorn Club. A fancy-pants gentlemen's club run by Wyoming's wealthy cattle barons.

Ox stretched out his arm, blocking Wyatt's path. "You told the sheriff you'd stay clear of trouble."

No, the problem was, trouble always found him. But this was a matter of doing what was right. Cliffton was a hazard to himself and his family. Miss Cathryn needed a champion. And Miss Jewel would get her lucky coin back.

Chapter Five

The peace and quiet of Northern Wyoming and Sweet Creek Ranch felt a million miles away from Cheyenne. Electric streetlights had replaced the gas lamps. Lights shone brightly in the windows of the colorful turrets, balconies, and gables making up the Longhorn Club. A couple dressed in frills posed for a photographer's camera on fan-shaped stone steps of a wide-welcoming veranda.

The tales Wyatt would have to tell. But to who? Not his family. Who knew when he'd see them or the ranch again. He scrubbed his eyes, making the irritation worse, not better.

A trio of men wearing fancy-embroidered shirts and large shiny belt buckles approached from the opposite direction. Blending in behind them, Wyatt climbed the steps of the Longhorn Club like he had every right to be there.

A squat man with a handlebar mustache fiddled with the insides of the camera box mounted atop a wooden tripod. "The readers of the *Daily News* can't get enough photos of Cheyenne's favorite rodeo stars."

The men tipped their hats. "The women and whiskey won't wait," one said as they strolled on.

One covered his face with his cowboy hat. "My wife will kill me if she learns I'm at the gaming table again."

Wreathed in lingering photo-flash smoke, the photographer was studying Wyatt extra close. "I know you from somewhere." He snapped his fingers. "You're that cattle rustler, with the last name of…wait, give me a minute and it will come to me."

Wyatt smiled, but kept walking. If he was going to catch up to Cliffton and the gold coin, he couldn't afford to linger.

A muscled fellow guarded the double doors, inset with frosted glass windows with a dandy painting of cowboys and Longhorn steers on a cattle drive. "Nice ride, Dusty," the guard said his voice a deep rumble. He allowed the rodeo stars to pass, but his brick-like hand thudded against Wyatt's chest. "Where do you think you're going? The club is for members only."

Wyatt feinted right, then left, then offered up a winning grin. In his experience, even the toughest thugs were susceptible to a full-force charm offensive. "Do I look like someone who would try to sneak in where I don't belong?"

A roomful of Quakers couldn't have looked grimmer. "There's always a joker in the crowd."

The pop from a champagne bottle and laughter spilled through the door. Wyatt's *aw-shucks act* never failed him. "Me and the boys had a bet. How am I gonna win if can't get inside for a quick look-see?"

The guard crossed his arms against his massive chest. "Not my problem."

A middle-aged woman displaying an abundance of diamonds and cleavage sashayed toward them with a feral glint in her makeup-laden eyes. "Tony, don't be a brute. Allow the sweet boy inside. He can be my guest."

Tony scowled. "Of course, Mrs. Morton."

"What, you're not calling me Charlotte these days?" Red fingernails stroked the guard's cheek. "Don't be a sourpuss. You know my dear husband encourages me to make friends."

Next she latched onto Wyatt's arm and pressed close. "What is your name, dear boy?"

"Wyatt, ma'am."

"Call me Charlotte."

"Hoo wee, that's a right friendly of you," he said, grabbing the wandering hand that squeezed his buttocks.

Tony narrowed his eyes at Wyatt. "If you cause any problems…"

"We'll behave ourselves. Ain't that so, Charlotte?" Mrs. Morton's amorous attentions while he hunted down Cliffton presented more of a danger than ten muscled guards.

Trilling laughter as her answer, she guided Wyatt into a ballroom dominated by a crystal chandelier and gold peacock wallpaper. Tux-wearing cattle barons, bankers, and lawyers stood in small groups looking stuffy and self-important. A few were accompanied by decades-younger bejeweled women sporting curve-revealing gowns.

Charlotte snagged two champagne flutes from a waiter,

and pushed one into Wyatt's hand. "Sweet boy, do you have a pleasure or sin that needs itching?"

Standing out like a hog in a horse paddock in his leather vest and denim shirt and pants, Wyatt glanced at the hall's multiple sets of paneled doors. The search for Cliffton might take more time than he'd calculated. "Could we start with those high-stakes gaming rooms I heard tell of?"

Charlotte's lipstick-smudged lips curved upward. "A gambler. I should have guessed."

One of the panel doors opened and Beau Blackwell strutted in with a busty blond draped on his arm.

Wyatt blinked. He had to be seeing things. Why wasn't Blackwell at home, entertaining Miss Cathryn?

"Don't get hot and bothered over Tammy," Charlotte said, clinging tighter to Wyatt's arm.

"Is she Blackwell's sister or cousin?" Wyatt didn't hold out much hope for a satisfactory answer.

Charlotte huffed. "That strumpet? Look at her glowing with smugness. The foolish woman believes the title of mistress will garner her some sort of respect. Just because you lavish jewels and furs on a cow, that doesn't make the cow the queen of England."

Stomach souring, Wyatt untangled himself from Mrs. Morton's clutches. "My ma used to say it was impossible to sling mud without getting dirty yourself."

"You're defending a strumpet?"

"Why aren't you lambasting Beau Blackwell?"

The bangles on Mrs. Morton's wrist clanged like cymbals as she flapped a dismissive hand. "Men will be men."

Tammy showed off a ring on her finger to Blackwell's cattle baron friends, and they shared a long kiss to enthusiastic hoots and whistles.

"Real men don't disrespect their woman," Wyatt said, gnashing his teeth and striding toward Blackwell.

"Sweet boy, where are you charging off to?" Mrs. Morton called.

Confronting Blackwell was exactly the type of brash move Wyatt had sworn off, but he couldn't turn away any more than a speeding bullet could be recalled once the trigger was pulled.

Blackwell saw him coming, and couldn't pedal backward fast enough. In his haste to escape, he ripped Tammy's mink cape from her shoulders.

Tammy yelped, then looked around confused. "Beau honey, what's wrong?"

Wyatt charged past her, zeroing in on his target.

Backed up against the peacock-papered wall, Blackwell brandished the white fur cape like a matador fending off a bull. "Who let you inside the club?"

Wyatt swiped the cape aside. "Go home and I won't squash you like a cockroach."

Tammy swatted Wyatt with a rhinestone-studded purse. "Leave him alone, you big oaf."

Nervous laughter rippled through the hall.

Murder burned in Blackwell's eyes. "Someone get the sheriff."

The gussied-up gathering relished the spectacle with the eagerness of country bumpkins rooting on the greased-pig contest.

If Wyatt was going to get arrested, he might as well make it worthwhile. He snagged a tablecloth from a nearby table, upending a vase of red roses.

Tammy squawked the loudest over the spray of water and crash of porcelain.

Before Blackwell knew what hit him, Wyatt had yanked the bulky man close, wrapped him mummy-like in the tablecloth, and tossed him over his shoulder.

Blackwell kicked and bucked. "Put me down!"

Wyatt strode for the exit, unable to leave quick enough. This might be the most lame-headed move in a long line of harebrained stunts.

Tammy dogged him, cussing foul enough to make a company of soldiers blush. "We'll make him pay for this."

Rearranging their clothing, Charlotte and Tony emerged from an alcove beside the frosted double doors.

"Tony, do something useful besides wiping lipstick from your mouth," Blackwell yelled, squirming harder.

In danger of dropping his load, Wyatt hoisted Blackwell higher and bolted outside. Halfway across the veranda, Tony latched onto his arm and dragged him to a stop.

"Drop him, or I'll wallop you a good one," Tony ordered.

Tammy beat Wyatt's arm with the rhinestone-studded purse. "Beau honey, hang on."

"Fire!" someone shouted from a short distance away.

Everyone turned toward the voice.

A bright flash blinded Wyatt. He blinked against the dark spots.

His vision slowly cleared, and he found himself staring at the man with the handlebar mustache. The photographer smiled and patted the camera box. "Thank you, Mr. Haven, for providing tomorrow morning's front page picture for the *Daily News*."

Wyatt dipped his shoulder and deposited Blackwell onto the porch floor. Then he advanced on the photographer. "I'm going to need to destroy that picture."

Tony and some other heavy-handed men grabbed hold of Wyatt.

He struggled, but couldn't shake them off. "Mister, you can't print that photo."

The handlebar mustache rose with the photographer's smile like a bird taking flight. "Tomorrow's society page will be the talk of Cheyenne."

"I'm going to destroy you, Wyatt," Blackwell barked, kicking and twisting, while Tammy worked to free him from the tablecloth. "I swear on my grave you will pay."

Wyatt stomped on Tony's foot. "Order someone to take away his camera instead of threatening me."

Tony slugged Wyatt.

His head snapped back. Eyes fluttering against the stinging pain and blood streaming from his nose, he was occupied with recovering his wits as the photographer gathered up the camera and tripod. The man raced down the stairs and disappeared into the dark.

Sheriff Judd and a posse of deputies arrived in cavalry-like fashion, with Garrett, Ox, and Billy hot on their heels.

"What did you do this time, Wy?" Ox asked.

The matter of fact tone and the lack of surprise on his,

Garrett's, and Billy's faces sliced deep as the lash of a whip. Why would they be shocked? Wyatt excelled at messing up. They expected him to clown about it, but his heart wasn't in it. "I stepped in it good this time, boys."

His need to show off had gotten Calvin killed. And his rash actions tonight had made Miss Cathryn's situation worse instead of better. When would he learn to mind his own business? The sooner he deserted the West and Wyoming the better it would be for everyone.

Chapter Six

Kitty swallowed the dry, tasteless toast and sipped the abysmally weak tea. Beau Blackwell's mansion was lovely, but the luxurious surroundings did not compensate for the fact her husband-to-be had not returned until the wee hours of the morning.

Consuela needed a lesson on the brewing of a proper pot of tea. While Kitty was at it, she should coax the stern woman to share some insight into the first Mrs. Blackwell, who had to be responsible for the elegant furnishings and tasteful wallpaper adorning the breakfast room. But she lacked enthusiasm for either task.

Mrs. Elaine Cliffton eyed her coddled egg with reproach. "Kitty, I do not know how you can eat when we know nothing of your brother's whereabouts."

Milton had undoubtedly spent his first night in Cheyenne pursuing debauchery of some sort. He would eventually find his way here, but not necessarily this day, or this evening.

Kitty was not surprised that the first favor she asked of Blackwell would involve rescuing her brother, but hated the fact anyway.

She dripped honey on a charred triangle of toast. "If we ate only when Milton was behaving himself, we would starve to death."

Mother jabbed the congealed yellow yolk with her fork. "How can you jest when your brother could be injured or dead?"

"My dear sister is the soul of thoughtfulness," Milton said, breezing into the room, a newspaper tucked under his arm. His eyes blazed bright, a good indication his latest slide into madness hadn't run its course.

Mother smiled wide, exposing molars strung together with gold fillings.

Kitty nibbled her toast. The combination of sweetness and charred crunchiness was at least tolerable. "You could have more compassion for your mother."

Emitting a mock gasp, Milton joined them at the breakfast table and slid the newspaper across the table. "I was expressly thinking of your and mother's welfare this morning. I thought it best to prepare you for a news article featuring your betrothed husband."

His jovial tone irritated. Kitty would not give him the satisfaction of appearing curious or worried. "Prepare us?"

Milton fished inside his breast pocket and dug out the snuffbox. "The local gossips will undoubtedly swoon with delight over the unseemly affair."

Mother's joy wilted. "Milton dear, I wish you would heed the doctor's advice to use your medicine in judicious amounts."

Milton's eyes went flat. "Don't, Mother." Dabbing the

coca-laced snuff to his nose, he snapped the small box closed.

Mother strangled her napkin. "Dear, I cannot help but worry when your health is so precarious. Kitty, beg your brother to be more cautious. Warn him that staying out all night is a tax upon his fragile system."

Kitty did not know the speed with which others grew a cold heart, but hers had been a long and winding journey. The roots could be traced back to the need to back out of her first polo tournament so Milton could be rescued from another gaming den. She had held out hope his bad behavior had peaked when Milton suffered a bad reaction to his *new medicine* and almost died on the eve of her first ball. The desultory affair carried on with the young men and girls moping over the cancellation of the dancing and the endless line of guests asking after her brother's and mother's welfare. Her despair deepened when Milton was accused of stealing the family heirloom snuffbox from the queen's second cousin.

Multiple witnesses confirmed the theft, but Milton denied the charge with vehemence. No formal charges were filed, but the family's disgrace could not have been more complete. Invitations to balls and banquets ceased. Kitty managed to save her tears for the privacy of her bedroom after their membership in the Somerset Polo Club was rescinded. Kitty's hasty engagement to the American cattle baron and their flight to America had been a necessary evil.

To add insult to injury, Mother's undying faith in her precious son reached new heights. Insisting Milton was suffering from the jealousies and lies of his peers, Mother berated Kitty for not having compassion on her brother, even as she admonished her to stop moping over the need to sell off all but a few of her ponies. Milton never apologized for the trouble or offered a single word of solace.

Kitty hoped, more than believed, that her brother was innocent of the theft. The end felt inevitable. The one small corner in her heart that held out hope for his redemption had iced over for good when he had nonchalantly produced the stolen snuffbox as their American-bound ship steamed out of port and asked them to admire his new *medicine* holder.

Kitty was the only one who spoke the truth. Not that it ever did any good. She said nothing now.

Mother teared up. "Is a little support too much to ask for?"

Most days Kitty managed to interact civilly with her family. "Forgive my rudeness, Mother." The warning about the gossips had her agitated. She had comforted herself the past few months with the belief that life in America would hold less drama.

Milton tapped the corner of the *Cheyenne Daily News*. "Page three is the one you want. The picture quality is horrible, but the amusing caption makes up for it."

Gathering her courage, she peeled back the inky, thin sheets. And swallowed.

Sensational did not begin to describe the half-page article. If she were not tangled up in the matter tighter than a fly in a web, she would find the piece highly entertaining.

Beau Blackwell hung upside down over Wyatt Haven's shoulder. A middle-aged woman, showing an indecent amount of cleavage, hit Haven with a foot-long clutch. Then there was the undeniably clever title.

CATTLE RUSTLER HOGTIES CATTLE BARON

Kitty was not angry, unnerved, or even surprised.

Instead, she wished Haven would walk through the door, throw her over his muscled shoulder, and carry her off to his ranch. What was the name...Sweet Creek Ranch? It sounded heavenly.

Horse hooey! That's what Father would say. *Don't need anyone, Kitty-Girl. Fend for yourself.* How many times had he repeated those and similar sentiments?

She refolded the newspaper and pushed away from the table. "I need to check on my ponies."

"You are going out in public?" Mother asked, aghast.

Milton chuckled. "Kitty will feel right as rain after having a good cry with her ponies."

Kitty hurried from the room. Time with her ponies did calm her, particularly when exchanges with her mother and brother proved vexing. Afterward she would confront Blackwell and seek an explanation for the scandalous picture.

Chapter Seven

Kitty ran into her husband-to-be as she headed out of the breakfast room.

Beau Blackwell caught her in his arms. "Slow down, woman."

She wrenched free. "I would like to speak to you in private."

Dark bags showed under his eye. "It'll have to wait. I'm on my way to the stockyard to meet some men about a contract."

The sooner she disabused him of the notion he could hide from her in plain sight the better. "I will walk with you. I want to check on my ponies."

Milton joined them. "Mind if I tag along?" No surprise there. Whether as a spectator or as a participant, her brother loved a good scandal.

Blackwell's mustache sagged. "Very well."

As Cheyenne woke to the embarrassing photo splashed across the society page, Kitty walked down an avenue bustling with merchants, cowboys, and school children. She held her head high against the stares, laughs, and whispers.

"Rules must be established regarding mistresses and lovers." She was proud of herself for maintaining a steady voice amid her disappointment and distress.

Her parents, like many who married for financial or family obligations rather than for love, had looked the other way at each other's many infidelities. It was the way of the rich and powerful. Kitty had so hoped hers would be a real marriage.

"Pray tell, what other rules do you expect your husband to abide by?" Milton asked, amused.

Kitty would not be thrown off task by Milton's callowness. "Discretion is a must."

Blackwell wore a pasted-on grin and tipped his hat at passersby. "I broke it off with Tammy."

Kitty's face ached from the effort to maintain her own fake smile. "If you are going to lie, you must do better than that."

Milton hooted. "Bravo, Kitten."

Blackwell gave her a sideways glance. "Wyatt Haven will pay for shaming me in front of the entire city."

Did all men dodge the blame for their own actions? How cynical of her. There had been no guile in Haven's brilliant blue eyes. He wouldn't lie or make excuses. What of her humiliation? "Am I to receive no apology?"

He smoothed his limp mustache. "I promise there won't be another whiff of scandal. We'll marry this afternoon and head to my ranch. By the time we return to Cheyenne, the gossips will be caterwauling over something new."

Americans had a reputation for being quick to forgive and forget indiscretions. That was something to be thankful for. The sooner she adapted and embraced her new life the better. "I do not suppose my presence would be welcomed at the Longhorn Club?"

Blackwell her for a long minute. "Many women find the atmosphere in a gentleman's club distasteful. If you could stomach the unseemly aspects, having you on my arm would be an asset."

The smell of manure and the lowing of thousands of cattle permeated the air as they approached the barn housing her ponies. A little dirt never killed anyone, Kitty-Girl, she lectured herself. "It is probably best to wait until we return in the fall to make our debut at your club."

Blackwell freed a red bandanna from his back pocket and dabbed his receding hairline. "The Double B Ranch is isolated. The closest neighbor is fifteen miles away. There's very little entertainment to be had. But you would find the Cheyenne summer insufferably hot."

Isolation suited Kitty. "Days spent training and caring for my ponies is all the entertainment I need."

Blackwell's eyes lighted, erasing ten years from his face. "You and my daughter will get on famously. I regret she won't be here for the wedding, but my Caroline insists on spending the winter snowbound at the Double B, spoiling her horses. And I never can say no to my baby girl."

Kitty took comfort in knowing her husband-to-be was not totally devoid of affection. But it did not erase the fact that his *baby girl* was only three years younger than she was. Certain to be an awkward situation for them both. Kitty planned to go out of her way to be agreeable and to cause as little trouble as possible. She could hope only that her stepdaughter would meet her halfway. "I am eager to meet Caroline."

Milton fiddled with his vest pocket. "We hear the young woman is quite lovely."

They entered the stuffy confines of the barn. Blackwell clapped Milton on the back. "Cliffton, there must be a way to convince you to travel north and visit the Double B. Surely your visit to New York City can wait?"

Milton directed a sly smile at Kitty. "Would you like Mother and me to extend our stay?"

Mr. Blackwell would be disappointed if he held hopes of his daughter and her brother forming an alliance. A poor horseman, with no love for dusty stables or sweat-inducing work, Milton would not last two months on a remote cattle ranch. Whereas Kitty couldn't wait to escape civilization.

She ignored the taunt in favor of pushing the sliding barn door open wider to allow for more light and air. "Good morning, my babies."

The ponies nickered and bobbed their heads.

Milton wrinkled his nose. "Please tell me the inspection of the ponies will not take long."

Relieved her ponies were holding up well after the rigors of the long journey, she knew their health and well-being still required close supervision. She stopped at the first stable box. Lord Braveheart sniffed her pocket where she usually kept treats such as carrot nubs or apple slices. "You are always hungry, aren't you?"

Blackwell and Milton joined her.

"Why is his nose running?" Milton asked, voice tinged with distress.

"It is perfectly normal," Kitty assured him. Amid coping with an outbreak of equine influenza among her ponies last fall, she'd had all she could do to keep Milton from selling them. He had ascribed the horses' illness to a plot by government agents to ruin him. Shortly after that came the incident with the stolen snuffbox.

If her father had willed the ponies to her as he promised, she would not have to worry over the next unreasonable or nonsensical notion to enter Milton's mind.

Blackwell seized Lord Braveheart's halter and collected a sample of the nasal discharge. "It's clear, and a good thing too, because a party of cavalry officers will be coming by to have a look at the ponies."

Her pulse sped. "The Clifftons have never bred ponies for army service. Tell him, Milton."

Her brother walked down the line of stable boxes, inspecting the other ponies. He turned troubled eyes on her. "They all have runny noses."

She balled her hands. Screaming in frustration would be a waste of breath. "The dusty train car and cattle yard are to blame. The ponies are in perfect health."

Left cheek twitching, Milton dug inside his pocket for the snuffbox. "Mr. Blackwell, if I were you, I would sell this whole lot of ponies and start fresh."

Distaste showed on Blackwell's face. "That won't be necessary."

She whirled on him. "They are not your ponies...yet."

"You may handpick the colts who show the most promise," he said, using an insufferable *let's be reasonable* tone.

She hurried to Winnie's box. Compromise was not possible. "I will call off the wedding before allowing my ponies to serve as cannon fodder."

Impatience flickered in Blackwell's eyes. "The United States Army is not at war. And they are *my* horses, not yours. Or did your brother neglect to tell you he signed the horses over to me last night?"

A bash from a mallet would have been less painful. She looked to Milton for confirmation. "Father promised the ponies to me."

Milton fumbled the snuffbox open. Studiously avoiding her eyes, he dabbed a pinch of the coca-laced snuff to his nostril and sniffed deeply. "Playing with ponies is for girls. You are a woman now and must turn your attention to raising a family."

If anyone needed straightening out, it was not her. "You sound just like Mother."

Winnie and the other ponies pranced and neighed with their ears perked, searching for the danger they sense in her voice.

Hand trembling, Kitty stroked Lady Winsome's neck. "Calm down, girl. There's no need to be afraid." Except fear, anger, and frustration coursed sickeningly through her veins. "I want to see the contract. There *is* a contract?"

"Why the fuss?" Blackwell asked. "It's a matter of simple math. There's a steady profit to be made selling horses to the army."

She clutched his sleeve. "Allow me full control of the ponies and I promise you will not regret it."

Blackwell shook free. "Don't get yourself all worked up."

The cajoling tone set her teeth on edge. "I remind you, I am a breeder of renown in polo-pony circles."

"You're in America now."

He might as well have told her to shut up. She glared at Milton. "Find a way to undo the contract, or—"

"What is done is done." He escaped through the barn door, practically running over a small contingent of military officers.

Her heart thundered like a herd of charging ponies. "Send them away."

Blackwell leveled a stern look at her. "Listen to your brother." He turned and greeted the cavalry officers.

Kitty would not make a scene. Unlike her brother, she detested public drama. But Mr. Blackwell was greatly mistaken if he believed he had won or interpreted her silence for acceptance of defeat.

The officers crowded around Lady Winsome's box. "How come this filly and the others haven't had their tails docked?" one of them asked.

"My farrier will see to it later today," Blackwell answered.

Kitty stifled a gasp. Composing herself, she hurried out of the stable. She wasn't going to allow her beautiful ponies to be cruelly mutilated.

Less than twenty minutes later, Kitty retrieved her hair brush from an ornate bedside-table and stuffed it into her gold brocade travel bag. Having changed into riding breeches and boots, she paced to the window.

There were no gardeners toiling in flower beds or horses trotting in green pastures. Cheyenne was all noise and commerce. The new start she had hoped to make in America had turned into a nightmare.

Beau Blackwell cared only about money, and Milton was riddled with delusions and paranoia.

The question was how would she make her escape from Cheyenne with her ponies? She could not and would not fail, but felt paralyzed by the daunting task.

The image of Wyatt Haven at the train station with a lasso twirling over his broad shoulders came to mind again. She had admired his competent yet gentle handling of Lady Winsome. His soothing presence had worked on Kitty as well. That was until she became dazzled by his sparkling blue eyes and gorgeous smile.

"Kitty, I must speak to you," Mother said, rapping on the door.

Kitty buttoned up the travel bag, shoved it under the bed, and opened the door "Come in."

Mother swept into the room, attended by a cloud of perfume. "I do not understand why you are angry with your brother."

Kitty was determined to act with patience during these last few moments together. It might be weeks or months before she reunited with Mother and Milton. "The ponies were to be my wedding present."

Mother hurried to the window, pulled the velvet drape aside, and peered up and down the street. "Why did you not insist that Milton return to rest?"

Mother's over-riding concern would be for Milton. Some things never changed. "Milton should not have sold the ponies without consulting me."

Mother snapped open her fan. "I do not understand the fuss. All your property goes to your husband upon marriage anyway."

Kitty should be used to her mother's indifference, but her attitude and harsh words cut deep just the same. "Do you always have to defend Milton?"

Mother batted the fan. "I sent Consuela out to purchase headache powder for Milton. I will send her back to the druggist to find something for your nerves."

Mother and Milton were maddeningly predictable. "I do not have a nervous condition. You both know how I feel about my ponies."

Her mother's brow furrowed. "You must marry Mr. Blackwell. Milton is not well enough to traipse all over the country in search of a new husband."

"I can take care of myself." That was what Father would expect her to say.

Consuela appeared in the doorway. "Should I place the headache medicine in Mr. Cliffton's room?"

Mother held up her fan as reply to Consuela. To Kitty, she said, "It is plain selfish to put your ponies' welfare above that of your family" She sailed out of the room.

Consuela cast a curious look at Kitty. "Would you like the door open or closed?"

Kitty sighed. "Closed, please."

Winnie and the other ponies gave her purpose and made the days bearable. She would send a telegram to Mother when she reached Henrietta's mountain ranch. Kitty and Henrietta were best of friends, exchanging letters regularly after Henrietta married an American and moved to Wyoming. Kitty hated to drag Henrietta into her problems, but knew she would be welcomed.

Making her escape posed a difficulty.

Wyatt Haven's brilliant smile filled her vision again. *If you get an itch to be a runaway bride, Miss Cathryn, please call on me for help. I promise you Beau Blackwell won't find our trail.*

The words were said in jest, but....

Haven was a cattle rustler. She could not ask for more experienced help if she was going to sneak her ponies out of town. He was her best hope.

There was only one way to learn if he would assist her. She donned her black top hat decorated with a brown satin ribbon matching her velvet riding habit, retrieved the travel bag from under the bed, and rushed out of the room.

"Where are you going?" Mother asked, coming out of Milton's bedroom.

Kitty paused beneath the hallway's glittering chandelier. "Errands."

"Why are you carrying your travel bag?"

Kitty froze. But the conversation quickly moved on to Mother's concern for Milton. "Oh, while you are out, could you look for a shop selling pillows? The ones on your brother's bed are far too soft."

Kitty kissed her mother's cheek. "I wish you would spend more care for yourself."

Spotting the maid exiting Milton's room with an armload of sheets, Mother hurried away. "Consuela, do not forget to use the lavender soap. Only lavender will do."

Kitty wished she had not been pushed into a corner. She could spend the rest of her days living her life for her uncaring mother and brother and husband-to-be or she could do what was best for herself and her ponies.

Heeding her heart, the choice became easy. She fled down the grand staircase, burst past the painted-glass doors, and lifted her face to the warm rays of the sun.

Chapter Eight

A Hereford bull's tail swished close to Wyatt's chin. He pushed on the bull's rump, directing the red and white animal toward the loading ramp.

Soot smearing his forehead, the engineer of the twelve o'clock train passed Wyatt as he walked the line of cattle cars, warning cowboys and ranchers to have their livestock loaded within the hour. He smirked. "Did Miss Tammy's purse leave bruises?" The man laughed uproariously. "Funniest picture in the newspaper in a long time."

Wyatt tipped his Stetson. The morning had been full of strangers cracking jokes at his expense. "Happy to do my part to entertain the fine citizens of Cheyenne."

In truth, he'd hardly slept a wink because of this latest mess-up. Thunderation! Miss Cathryn had to be suffering ridicule and embarrassment thanks to his idiocy. It was high time he learned to control his foolish impulses.

Ox rested his ham-hock arms on a cow's rump and shook his head. "That Tony fellow busted your face good. How long you gonna talk funny?"

Wyatt touched his tender swollen nose. "Last time I

talked funny for two days."

Ox grinned. "Some folks don't know how to take a joke."

Billy, whose freckles were becoming more vivid with each passing day in the sun, threw away the long straw of hay he'd been chewing on. "I can't wait to tell Mr. Ty and Mr. Boone about you hogtying Blackwell."

Garrett waded through the milling cows with a smile on his face. "Did Beau Blackwell smell like a goat while you were carrying him like a sack of potatoes over your shoulder?"

Wyatt's conscience kicked. The boys laughing over another one of his foolhardy stunts reinforced his decision to leave Wyoming. "Actually, he smelled like the back end of that old sow who used to squeal up a racket and chase me onto the porch."

Ox grinned wider. "You would run like your pants were on fire."

Billy cast a hopeful look at Wyatt. "You could come back to Sweet Creek Ranch. We can't tell stories as funny as you can."

In the wake of the killing winter of 87, Wyatt had been forced to leave Sweet Creek. But then he knew the absence wouldn't be for good. This time was different. Today might be the last time he laid eyes on Garrett, Ox, and Billy.

He glanced at the brick clock tower. Less than an hour's worth of wisecracking and he'd be able to lick his wounds in private. In the meantime, he'd keep these boys smiling even if he had to drop down on all fours and bark like a dog or use his goo-goo, gaga baby routine.

Taking a deep breath, Wyatt screwed up his face like he'd bitten into a lemon. "You just want to watch Mr. Ty and Mr. Boone put a dunce cap on me."

Billy grinned. "Did you have to sit in the corner all the time when you were in school?"

"It's not something to brag on." Wyatt's parents were pioneers who'd died on the Oregon Trail, leaving him an orphan at fourteen. He'd gotten an education of a different sort when he hooked up with a cattle-rustling outfit.

A rambunctious heifer bumped up against him. Patting the cow's curly white forehead, he got the surprise of his life upon spotting Miss Cathryn Cliffton hurrying toward him. The hungry male side of his brain noted the breeches hugging her womanly curves. But the determined look on her face set off alarm bells.

He needed to apologize. But to say what? Sorry for the humiliating photo. Sorry your husband-to-be has a mistress. Sorry your brother is a pompous bore and a thief.

A wake of snickers and gossip dogged her steps, but her coffee-colored eyes remained glued on him.

"You're in big trouble," Ox said with a grin.

"I'll catch up with you boys before the train leaves." Wyatt set out on a crash course with Miss Cathryn.

Sleek brown hair framed her face beneath the brim of her fancy top hat. "Mr. Haven, would you do me the favor of—"

"Meet me behind Hopkins's Stables," he said, brushing past her.

He didn't turn back at her gasp of dismay. He had no

intention of cheating her out of the blistering rebuke he deserved, but a public quarrel wouldn't help her cause.

Circling around the long way to the stables at a fast clip, he arrived the back door of the livery just as Miss Cathryn rounded the opposite corner.

She sure was pretty with the pink blush feathering her high cheekbones and the lively glint in her eyes. He removed his white Stetson and finger-combed his hair. Where to start his apology? "Miss Cathryn, I—"

"How kind and fast thinking of you, Mr. Haven, to arrange a private meeting" she said in a gentle tone. "This quiet spot suits my purposes perfectly."

His jaw went slack. "You're not angry?"

She bit her lip. "I was about to make the biggest mistake of my life. I have you to thank for opening my eyes to Mr. Blackwell's true nature."

Wyatt wasn't sure what to make of the unexpected turn. Should he mention that he'd seen her brother steal the Jewel of Texas's lucky gold coin? And he wished she'd stop worrying her full lip as it was an unwanted distraction. "I'm right happy for you, ma'am. But I'm a might confused over why you'd want to meet with me. Actually, I'd feel better if you stormed at me some."

She looked briefly unsettled, then drew back her slim shoulders. "You said I could call on you if I wanted to be a runaway bride."

The sun shining in his eyes and the breeze slapping his face were too real for her words to be a dream. "Aren't you supposed to be dressed in your wedding gown and standing at the altar before you can be called a runaway bride?"

Her eyes narrowed. "Were you jesting, or is it possible to escape without Beau Blackwell being able to follow my trail? Before you answer, you should know I want to sneak away with Lady Winsome and five more of my polo ponies."

Holy smokes, she was serious. And people called *him* crazy. The only place he could think of to take her would be impossible and dangerous. "I can't take you to Hole-in-the Wall. It ain't a fit place for women, never mind an English lady like yourself."

Doubt crept into her eyes. "Would my ponies be safe there?"

The horses would be perfectly safe. But outlaws of all stripes regularly used Hole-in-the-Wall as a hideout. "Cattle rustlers and bank robbers ain't exactly friendly."

She exhaled sharply. "I will take my chances."

"Whoa up. Just you slow down." She gazed at him expectantly. Dang it! When would he learn to keep his big mouth shut? His foolish antics had gotten young Calvin killed. Wyatt would slit his own throat before allowing someone else to get hurt or die because of his stupidity. "Why the drastic measures? Call off the wedding. Go back to England."

Her eyes clouded. "I cannot do that."

There had to be a way to make her see reason. "Blackwell hates my guts. That won't do your cause any good."

She folded her hands. "My brother sold my ponies to Beau Blackwell, so technically we will be stealing them."

The trouble just kept piling up. "There's no technically about it. Horse theft is a hanging offense." That was a bit of an exaggeration. For a first-time offense, he'd be more likely to go to prison. Unless he got the wrong judge.

Her beautiful face paled. "Forget I asked, Wyatt."

If she'd called him Mr. Haven, he might've stood a chance of watching her go. A small, small chance. Besides it was plain as day, she was determined to go through with this hare-brained scheme with or without him. "I can help you escape with your ponies." He would bet his last dollar she wasn't in the habit of acting on the spur of the moment. "We can't stay at Hole-in-the-Wall forever."

She nodded. "Do you know Rosewood Ranch?"

"It sits fairly close to Hole-in-the-Wall."

"Henrietta Rochester is a good friend. She and her husband will assist me in purchasing the ponies from Mr. Blackwell."

He gripped her arm. It was long and delicate, but overlaid with toned muscle. "That's a three-hundred-mile journey north."

"My ponies are strong."

He admired her courage, but would have preferred her to be discouraged or daunted by the difficulties of the journey ahead. "We can take the train most of the way." He'd need his brothers' help to smuggle the horses aboard the train. Shoot! They were going to put up a squawk when they learned of this latest escapade.

He checked the clock tower. Fifty more minutes before the train pulled out of the station. The short deadline might make her think twice. "But we need to go now. The element of surprise will better our chances of making a clean escape."

"My bag is packed and hidden in the stockyard stable." Like a filly kicking up her heels, she pulled free of his grip and raced away.

Thunderation. Wasn't she something? Full of one surprise after another.

His blood hummed in that old familiar way. He did love a good adventure. Not to mention relishing the idea of keeping close company with Miss Cathryn. Imagine that, a common cowpoke like him keeping company with a society lady. What would the gossips say?

His step hitched. An unmarried, unchaperoned woman couldn't traipse off with men who weren't her kin. She'd be called a floozy or worse. Her chances of making a respectable marriage would be ruined.

He'd eat his Stetson before he allowed that to happen.

Where did that leave them?

He could call the whole escape off. Or...he and Miss Cathryn could marry.

Whoa doggie! If he followed through on the ridiculous notion, everyone would think he was plunging down the crazy stream with a boat full of holes.

Chapter Nine

Leaving Wyatt Haven behind, Kitty weaved her way through the bustling stockyard. Spotting Beau Blackwell exiting the barn stabling her ponies with the army officers on his heels, she ducked behind a hay wagon. Her heart beat rapidly and a cold sweat dampened her forehead. The audacious plan to escape with the ponies in broad daylight felt more like a dream than real.

Haven joined her, his wide chest and shoulders crowding her as he crouched down to conceal his cowboy hat from sight. The scent of leather and man and straw was dizzying. She avoided the magnetic draw of his crystal blue eyes. "The leads for the ponies are stored in a crate beside the first stable box. Stay here, I will check to see if any of Mr. Blackwell's men are with my ponies."

Haven hooked her arm. "Hold up. Did you stop to think that an unmarried woman such as yourself can't go running off with a single man without a chaperone? At first, I thought we'd have to marry, but that won't be necessary if your ma or someone else accompanies us. Otherwise we have no choice but to get hitched."

Her mouth dropped open. "Marry? You and me? Us?"

He flashed a charming grin. "Yup, you will need to wed a nasty, no-good cattle rustler. That is, unless you find an appropriate travel companion. But I'm guessing Mrs. Elaine Cliffton wouldn't approve of you tromping off into the remote wilds of Wyoming with the likes of me. I could ask one of my brothers, but—"

"No." It wasn't fair to involve more people in her troubles.

His chiseled chin firmed. "Hogwash. I don't mind sticking my neck out to help you, but I won't be accused of sullying a woman's good name."

She growled in frustration. Of all the cattle rustlers in the West she would have to run into one with a conscience. "Marriage is a drastic measure. Surely we can find a simpler solution."

His blue eyes intent in thought, he rolled his muscled shoulders. "Once we get off the train in Aurora, I could probably convince Ugly Sally and Buck to come with us to Hole-in-the-Wall." He ticked points off on his fingers. "Ty and Ella can't leave the ranch. Boone is the sheriff, and by rights should arrest us. Maggie was a bounty hunter and would be a good candidate, except now she's a schoolteacher. Besides, Boone would bite my head off for my trouble. My brothers and sisters-in-laws are out. So, it will have to be Ugly Sally and Buck, but that won't help us now."

Kitty was touched by his genuineness. And couldn't help envying the love and fondness in his voice as he spoke of his family and friends. "Forgive me for trying to drag you into my troubles. It was selfish of me."

Haven frowned. "Don't chicken out on account of marrying me. You're making too big a deal out of it. We can divorce as soon as you're safe with your friends at the Rosewood Ranch."

Her attraction to him posed a danger. "Marriage and divorce are not as simple as buying and selling cattle."

"They are in Wyoming. Folks in a hurry to divorce travel here just for that reason. Our laws are on the lax side."

Impatience bubbled up. "You are not going to budge unless we marry?"

"You got that right, ma'am."

Wyatt Haven was her best hope for escaping with her ponies. He was assuming a huge risk to aid her. She sighed. "How do we go about finding someone to marry us on such short notice?"

His blue eyes softened. "Don't look so sad."

"Did you ever wish life was simpler?"

"I prefer it to be interesting."

She sighed again. "You must be delighted with how this day is going."

He stuck his finger up his nostril and twisted his finger in exaggerated fashion, pretending to pick his nose. "It could be worse. You could be marrying a toothless gold miner or a banjo-playing sod buster."

She tugged his arm down. "Don't do that."

He grinned. "We're not even married and you're already bossing me around."

Her face heated. "You appear to need it."

"Yes, ma'am."

"We come to say goodbye," said a husky young man, walking behind the hay wagon. A freckled-face, red-headed lad and a handsome cowboy with shy eyes accompanied him.

"Howdy, boys," Haven said affably. "This here is Miss Cathryn Cliffton."

He winked at her. "These clods are my brothers." Then his good humor evaporated. "I'll introduce everyone later, but right now Miss Cathryn is in desperate need of our help."

Kitty wanted to protest his characterizing her situation as desperate. Urgent sounded more dignified, but she could not deny the clawing nature of the distress eating at her insides.

Haven shoved a handful of money at the red-headed lad. "I need you to go to the ticket office and buy us two train tickets. We will be traveling to Aurora with you."

Freckled face intent on his mission, the lad galloped off.

Haven thrust more bills at the beefy fellow. "Ox, locate a box car that will comfortably hold six horses."

Ox offered a doubtful look in return. "That's going to be a tall order on such short notice."

Haven clapped his burly shoulder. "Use some of that charm you been holding in reserve."

Rumbling with laughter, Ox headed off in the same direction as the red-headed youth.

The shy cowboy shuffled in place. "I'm almost afraid to ask what I'm supposed to do."

Haven grinned. "Garrett, I need you to be a witness at my wedding."

The stunned expression on Garrett's face was comical. "What have you gone and done this time, Wy?"

She hurried to Haven's defense. "Mr. Haven has acted like the noblest of gentlemen." If she set aside the nose-picking act, it was true.

Haven sobered. "You got to trust me on this one."

Garrett gave him a long look, then tipped his hat to her. "Welcome to the family, Miss Cathryn."

Her mouth went dry as sawdust. "Thank you, but the marriage is of a temporary nature."

"You don't think a proper lady would actually marry a country bumpkin like me?" Haven said. His large mitts clasped her waist. Lifting off her feet, he spun her in a circle, proving his point.

She slapped his bull-sized chest, but she was at the mercy of his brute strength and size. "Mr. Haven, what are you doing?"

His smile as wide as the outdoors, he set her on her feet. "Trying to cheer you up."

She gulped down air. "I do not need cheering."

Garrett wore a commiserating smile. "Wyatt means well. Just ignore it when he acts like an overgrown puppy, and he'll settle down."

Haven took her hand. "Time's a-wasting. Let's go find us a judge."

"Tally ho!" she muttered, allowing him to whisk her from behind the hay wagon. Fox hunting was not her sport of choice. The few times she had participated she found herself rooting for the fox. Trotting to keep up, she was full of empathy for the harried fox. Now she would be the one desperate to keep one step ahead of the hunters and hounds.

Before she could catch her breath, Kitty and Wyatt and Garrett Haven stood huddled in Judge Peck's cramped private chamber. Gravy stained the corner of the portly judge's mouth, due to the interruption of his noon meal. Though unhappy about parting with his bowl of pork stew, the judge quickly fell under the sway of Haven's out-sized charm and wit.

Wire-rimmed spectacles perched on the end of his bulbous nose, Judge Peck thumbed through a small black book. "We'll have to keep this short and sweet as I'll soon have a courtroom full of prostitutes to convict and sentence. Nothing gives you indigestion faster than weeping whores."

Haven glanced down at her. "Short and sweet suits us fine."

Us. Panic grabbed Kitty by the spine. Was she really trusting her future to a cattle rustler? Milton was reckless, whereas she was the responsible one. Marriage was not a change of clothes that one put on and off as the mood, temperature, and occasion suited. She would be ill at the hypocrisy if she had to repeat wedding vows. She gnashed on her lip. "Can we just sign our names, and be done with it?"

The judge looked at her over the top of his spectacles. "Excuse my impertinence, but brides usually look happy on their wedding day. Marrying this rascal to exact revenge on Beau Blackwell seems excessive."

Her face heated. She had been prepared to endure a brief spell in the limelight with the interest raised by the wedding. But not more scandal. Having suffered months of gossip and people talking behind her back every time she left her London home due to the accusation of theft levied at her brother, she was not ready to face the rabid curiosity arising from the sensational newspaper photo. Nor the uproar once word of her hasty marriage to Wyatt Haven got out. She could imagine the headlines.

ENGLISHWOMAN JILTS CATTLE BARON FOR CATTLE RUSTLER

or

CATTLE RUSTLER STEALS BRIDE AND SIX POLO PONIES

She cleared her constricted throat. "Revenge is the last idea I have in mind. Buxom Tammy is welcome to keep Mr. Blackwell."

Judge Peck chuckled. "I like your sass, little lady."

Shy-eyed Garrett, who had been silent, also laughed. "Wyatt needs a firm hand to keep him in line. Glad to see you're up to the task, ma'am."

Haven wagged his brows. "Don't go blabbing to Miss Cathryn about my bad habits."

She wished she had the ability to jest and joke in the face of disaster. But she could work on throwing Beau

Blackwell off their trail. "Mr. Haven and I are not sure where we should spend our honeymoon. We are torn between Mexico and California. Which do you suggest?"

The judge removed the wire-rimmed spectacles and rubbed his eyes. "I don't know what this charade is about, but I'm going to trust you two have good reasons for what you're doing."

Shame washed through her. Judge Peck was no fool and did not deserve to be treated as such. "Mr. Haven is kindly assisting me with a troublesome matter."

Judge Peck exhaled heavily. "Wyatt isn't exactly an expert on avoiding trouble."

Her nerves hummed excruciatingly.

The judge searched through the files cluttering his desk and slid out the one marked Marriage Licenses. "I hope you know what you're doing, miss."

Garrett brushed aside his bangs. "We gotta get a move on. I can't miss the train."

It was clear the judge and Garrett didn't approve of the proceedings. Who could blame them? "Please give us moment." She dragged Haven to the far corner.

His blue eyes twinkled like the night sky filled with fireworks. "I don't snore. But that's probably not what's worrying you."

The cramped corner grew smaller thanks to his mountainous presence. If he were a horse he'd be a Clydesdale. As with those gentle giants, he would not harm her. Not on purpose. But his rambunctiousness was a force to be reckoned with.

She pressed back against the crevice. "It's unfair of me

to tangle you up in my problems."

"It was either help you or join a traveling circus."

"Don't tease."

His smile faded. "I wish I was. But that's another kettle of beans. Are you positive your mother and brother can't help you with buying your horses back from Blackwell? That sure would save you a lot of trouble."

"Milton has it in his mind my ponies are going to get sick and die." Didn't that sound ridiculous? There was no time to explain Milton's paranoia and her mother's continual aiding and abetting of his delusions. And she would prefer to avoid the pain of laying bare said weaknesses and failings. "I cannot take the chance. Not with Mr. Blackwell planning to dock my ponies' tails." The mere thought made her ill. "I will not sit back and allow that to happen."

"I've helped castrate bulls and stallions, and I'm sure they'd have rather had their tails lopped off." Haven's voice could not have been more kind and gentle. "Is that why you're in such a rush to be off?"

Was there any way to say he wouldn't understand without it sounding petulant? London Bridge! Here she was judging her brother's and mother's follies while she counted her ponies as her closest friends and loved them more than family. She crossed her arms and lifted her chin. "Please excuse me, and I shall be on my way. And you can forget we ever met."

Haven's lazy cowboy bearing vanished, and his eyes locked on her. "Nope. Not gonna happen. I said I would help. And I will. Us Havens keep our promises. Ain't that right, Garrett?"

Sympathy shone in the young cowboy's eyes. "Ma'am, you'd have an easier time taking a bone from a Mastiff than shaking off Wyatt."

Judge Peck pointed to the marriage license sitting beside the bowl of congealing stew. "Sign your names or get going. Either way I'd like to finish my lunch in peace."

Haven held out his hand. "We need to be loading your ponies onto the train."

"Ma'am," the judge said impatiently.

She stared at a palm twice as wide as her own. He was using her one weakness against her. She took a breath and placed her hand in his. "God help us both," she whispered.

Leading her to the desk, he spoke in her ear. "Glad to know I'm marrying a prayerful woman."

His palm was callused from long hours of clasping reins. Which was oddly comforting. She found herself smiling. "Don't be surprised if you find yourself praying we never met."

He grasped the pen the judge pointed out. "Nope. Won't happen." Then he dipped the pen in the inkwell, signed the marriage license, and passed the pen to her.

He made the whole affair seem simple. Annoyed her hand was trembling she signed her name. Her neat and orderly signature was dwarfed by Haven's large, looping handwriting. She breathed a sigh of relief. There. It was done.

Judge Peck waved Garrett over. "Come add your John Hancock."

"Hold up," Haven said. "Don't I get to kiss my bride

first?"

Her pulse quickened and she stared at him. "K-k-kiss?"

Judge Peck cleaned his spectacles on his vest. "By all means."

"Make it fast," Garrett said as he signed the marriage license.

Before she could protest, Haven cupped her elbows, and his wide, firm mouth moved over her lips. Pulling her onto her tiptoes, he deepened the kiss.

"Mr. Haven!" She broke free and rubbed her mouth with the back of her hand. The taste of maple syrup lingered on her lips. "Was that necessary?"

He couldn't have looked prouder of himself. "All marriages are sealed with a kiss."

Her insides were a turbulent, molten mess. "Never do that again."

"We need to go," Garrett said, opening the door.

As Haven and Garrett hustled her out of the room, Judge Peck was shaking his head in amusement. "Best wishes, Mr. and Mrs. Haven."

Thankfully Haven and Garrett were supporting her. She was Mrs. Cathryn Haven. Wife of a cattle rustler. How had her life gone so off course? Would she find a way back to the life she was born to?

Her lips still tingled from the surprise kiss. What would she do if Wyatt Haven tried to kiss her again? Though she had rebuffed him, a corner of her heart rebelled, inciting the image of stealing more kisses from a wild-blooded cowboy.

Chapter Ten

Superb polo ponies exhibited calm amid chaos. Kitty's ponies proved they had the hearts of champions as she led Lady Winsome, Lord Braveheart, and her youngest pony, Duchess Lovey through the crush of pedestrians, cowpokes, carriages, and ox-drawn carts clogging the rail yard. Haven led the other three ponies.

The engine of the twelve o'clock train hissed and belched smoke. An eager-faced newsboy hawked the morning paper to the travelers boarding the railroad coach cars. But Haven could not have looked calmer, wearing the same happy-go-lucky expression as when they had waltzed the ponies out of the stables under the pretense of exercising them.

Meanwhile, her heart beat double time. She wanted to believe she would rest easier once they loaded her babies into the waiting boxcar and took their seats in the coach, but lying to oneself was so much horse hooey. Getting the ponies on the train would be the start of trouble, not the end.

Haven was not totally oblivious to the danger. After

collecting their train tickets and being pointed to the waiting livestock boxcar, he had instructed his brothers to board the train and to keep clear of the actual horse abduction.

She chewed on her lip. She did not view what she was doing as stealing. By rights, the ponies were hers.

"You're gonna chomp through your lip if you're not careful," Haven said, his drawl smooth as warm honey.

If Beau Blackwell possessed a smidgen of Wyatt Haven's gallantry, she would not have needed to ask a stranger to break the law. "I am usually very self-reliant. I should not have mixed you up in my problems." The lead ropes chafed the palms of her gloveless hands. "Help me load the ponies, and after that we can go our separate ways. Maybe you could give me your gun, and we can tell the authorities I forced you to help me at gunpoint."

Merriment shone in his crystal-blue eyes. "If it's all the same to you, I'd rather be strung up by the neck as a horse thief than having folks think I let a slim whip of a girl get the best of me."

"Be serious."

His mouth firmed. "Do you think anyone will believe you overpowered me?"

He had a point. He stood head and shoulders above everyone else and his broad chest was brick-wall solid. Her mouth dried. Was she really placing her welfare in the hands of this stallion of a man?

She reminded herself that the ponies' safety was all that mattered. She was rescuing them before Blackwell could do them harm. After that? She would just have to convince him to be a gentleman and sell the ponies to her.

She slapped her forehead. "London Bridge!"

Duchess Lovey danced at the end of her lead, her eyes widening. "Steady, girl," Kitty said in soothing tones, even as the full implications of the rushed marriage to Haven exploded through her mind in blinding fashion. If the document she had signed was legal—and she had no reason to believe it was not—that meant she would soon be in possession of her dowry. A sum of money generous enough to establish countless polo pony farms.

Haven stopped beside her. "London Bridge?"

The exclamation had been her father's favorite when excited or surprised. She bounced on her toes. "When this is over, I will be able give you a large reward." Every man had their price. Including Beau Blackwell. She was prepared to offer him a ransom's worth of money for her ponies.

Haven grasped her elbow. "I'm not doing this for money."

"Noble man," she grumbled, but was touched by his sincerity. "You will take the money for my sake. How else will I assuage my guilt for mixing you up in this mess?"

He shrugged, but his eyes remained clouded. "Pa Malcolm and Ma Viola taught all their boys to treat others the way you wanted to be treated. You'd help me if I was in trouble, wouldn't you?"

Caught off guard, she could only blink. She wished she could agree, but did not want to lie. Not to him. She gave unselfishly to her ponies. But would she be so generous with people? Especially a stranger? No, she did not possess the same amount of goodness he did.

"All aboard," the train engineer called. "Last call. All aboard."

"We best get a move on," Haven said gently.

A few minutes later the ponies were safe aboard the boxcar and had all the comforts they could hope for, since Haven's brothers had seen to providing fresh straw for bedding and secured water buckets to the wooden slats. She hugged her middle tighter as the railroad workers slid the boxcar doors closed.

Haven poked her with his elbow. "Come on, I'm hankering to carry my new bride over the threshold of the passenger car."

He wouldn't. Would he? The picture in the morning newspaper of Haven with Beau Blackwell slung over his shoulder came to mind. She pointed a warning finger. "Do not dare."

He snapped his fingers. His eyes held a mischievous twinkle. "Shucks. We've only been married a few moments and here you are ruining my fun."

"That will teach you not to marry in haste."

"That's better."

Keeping up with the swift change of directions of his mind was a full-time job. "What?"

"You're smiling."

She lifted her hand to her mouth. "I am?"

His white-toothed smile was blinding. "I hope you don't mind me saying smiles look right pretty on you."

Two quick toots from the conductor's whistle gave her a start. "If we don't hurry, we will miss our train."

Haven offered his elbow. "I'll shoot up the train if they try to leave without us."

He was only kidding she told herself as they dashed toward the passenger coach. At least she hoped he was joking.

A few steps from the train steps, Beau Blackwell stepped into their path, accompanied by several gun-toting cowboys and a lean man dressed in gray overalls. She guessed he was the farrier, probably on his way to the stables to dock her ponies' tails.

She stopped short, and gasped for breath. "Move aside, you fiends."

Haven freed his gun and used his body to shield hers. Tension vibrated through his taunt muscles, but his voice was deceptively calm. "We don't want no trouble."

Blackwell glowered at them from beneath the brim of his bowler. "Where do you think you're going with my bride?"

Haven's gun didn't waver, but remained squarely aimed at Blackwell's chest. "You can't be surprised Miss Cathryn decided to toss you aside for someone else after you embarrassed her in front of the whole city."

"Tossed me aside for *who*?" Blackwell's mustache twitched. "Don't tell me *you* married my bride. Not after humiliating me with that picture in the paper."

The train whistle screeched.

Kitty plugged her ears.

Haven didn't flinch. "If you'll excuse us we have a train to catch."

"Step away from my bride," Blackwell demanded,

seething with rage. "Unless you want Miss Cathryn caught in the crossfire."

Kitty's face heated. Was he actually threatening her? "Do not make the mistake of believing I am too genteel to make a scene." Years of living with Milton had made her an expert in the art of the dramatic. "I will scream murder if you lay one finger on me or Mr. Haven."

Haven grasped her hand and squeezed her fingers in a reassuring manner. He could not have looked calmer even though he was outgunned six to one. "Miss Cathryn, go take your seat on the train and I will join you soon."

The shrill call of the train whistle skittered down her spine. She held tighter to Haven's hand. If the train left without them, she would have the comfort of knowing her ponies would be safe. In the meantime, she would not abandon Wyatt Haven to Beau Blackwell's vengeance. "I am not leaving without you."

Haven glanced at her. "I like independent, strong-minded women, but I won't see you hurt or killed because of me."

She pointed an accusing finger at Blackwell. "If anything happens to me, it will be his fault not yours."

Blackwell's murderous gaze remained fixed on Haven. "The longer you drag this out the worse it'll be for you."

A crowd of onlookers gathered.

"Are you going to have Tammy hit me some more with her purse?" Haven asked straight-faced.

Raucous laughter filled the air.

Blackwell mangled the brim of his bowler. "We'll see how funny you think it is if I take a horsewhip to you."

The click of guns cocking came from behind them. Kitty spun around. An intense young man and a boy with a badly bruised face had their guns trained on Blackwell's men.

"Step aside," the young man said, the ferocity in his voice matching his stormy eyes. "And allow my brother and his lady friend to go on their way."

Haven groaned. "Don't get mixed up in this, Seth."

"Too late for that," Seth spit back.

The boy with the bruised face waved his heavy gun in careless fashion. "Mr. Seth is in a poor mood. You best listen to him."

The train lurched forward on creaking wheels.

Kitty was ready to burst from the tension. "Mr. Blackwell will not shoot us. Not with all these witnesses."

Blackwell signaled his men to lower their guns, and then narrowed his eyes at Haven. "You'll pay, if not today, then tomorrow, or the day after that."

The train rattled and chugged ahead.

Haven smiled. "You'll have to catch me first." Dragging her by the arm, he sprinted for the stairs of a passing coach car. He jumped for it and hauled her onto the lowest step.

His arms circled her in protective fashion. "Are you okay?"

Her heart beat dizzyingly fast. Her legs had turned to jelly. And her ankle hurt from landing wrong on it. "I feel wonderful." The elation she felt the first time she jumped a hedgerow on a pony came close. But marrying Wyatt Haven, smuggling her ponies aboard a train, and the standoff with Beau Blackwell had undoubtedly given her the most exciting day of her life.

Haven eyed her as if she were batty. "You best get some rest. You'll need it for the ride to Hole-In-The-Wall."

Her stomach twisted. It was too early to celebrate. They had miles to go yet. With bank robbers and cattle rustlers standing between her and sanctuary with Henrietta at Rosewood Ranch. Convincing Beau Blackwell to sell the ponies back to her might be more difficult that she anticipated, but she would figure out a way.

The stifling confines of the train stairwell closing around her, she broke free of Haven, and limped her way down the aisle of the packed coach.

As long as she had her ponies, all would be well.

Chapter Eleven

His broad-brimmed Stetson almost scraping the train ceiling as he made his way down the narrow aisle of the cramped passenger car, Wyatt pointed Miss Cathryn to the empty seats next to his brothers. Garrett, Ox, and Billy whistled and clapped at his and Miss Cathryn's narrow escape. Meanwhile, the other riders on the train wore cautious or confused looks, a natural response to the armed confrontation they'd just witnessed.

He smiled and nodded, to show them he was harmless. "How's that for your own personal Wild West show? We'd hoped to throw in some trick riding and fancy rope work for your enjoyment, but we ran out of time."

He was rewarded with nervous laughter and genuine grins. His brothers chuckled the loudest.

Miss Cathryn looked back at him in amazement. "I wish I had your talent for bouncing back from adversity."

Proper and polite as she was, she probably was holding back her true thoughts and was most likely wondering if he was an idiot who never kept his mouth shut. He shrugged. "I don't like seeing folks looking sad or out of sorts."

Her brow knitted. "Who put you in charge of making the world a happier—" The train lurched forward, almost toppling her.

He snagged her around the waist and pulled her against his body. Thunderation, but that felt good. Too good.

She squeaked in surprise and struggled against him. "Mr. Haven, let go of me."

Her squirming made him want to hold on tighter. His nose was drawn to her nape. She smelled real pretty. He released her before she clobbered him a good one. "What's that perfume you're wearing?"

Growling in frustration, she hobbled to the waiting bench and slid to the corner, tucking herself up against the window. She made quite the ravishing picture in her form-fitting outfit.

Was there a polite way for a man to tell a woman she made him drool? He dropped down next to Miss Cathryn, relishing the thought of having her company all to himself for the four-hour trip.

She jabbed him with her elbow. "Move over."

He crossed his arms, trying to make himself as small as possible, but unless he wanted to sit on the floor there was no way around rubbing shoulders with his new wife.

Seated across the aisle, his brothers guffawed.

As a rule, Wyatt always found something to smile about, but his day had gone to heck in a hurry. First the picture in the newspaper. Then the hasty marriage to Miss Cathryn. Stealing six horses. A near shootout at the train station.

And it was only noon.

The clacking of the train wheels reached a steady hum, and the city limits of Cheyenne gave way to unending miles of scrub brush.

Miss Cathryn exhaled a long breath and her frown eased. "Will he come after us? Me?"

If Blackwell didn't already hate him, he must now. He sighed. "This isn't the first time I've humiliated Blackwell. There was this big rodeo last fall. And I sort of lassoed him. And he was none too pleased."

Her interest perked. "Why did you lasso him?"

"He spoke disrespectful to Garrett."

She nodded encouragingly.

Wyatt squirmed in his seat. Lassoing Blackwell hadn't been his best moment. "Garrett's new barn had been burned to the ground."

"While he was at the rodeo?"

"No, a short time before."

"And you lassoed Blackwell as punishment?"

"No. It was the only way to get his attention." Embarrassing and irritating the heck out Blackwell had been a bonus. The explanation sounded lame to his ear. "You had to be there to understand. The Daltrey Gang were the ones who burned down Garrett's barn and clobbered him over the head and stole his cattle. But everyone knew who was behind it."

"What did Beau Blackwell have against Garrett?" she asked.

Wyatt rolled his shoulders. "He was hoping to run Garrett off his ranch."

"The Daltrey Gang." She glanced nervously out the window. "They sound like dangerous men. Milton warned me the West and Wyoming were overrun with outlaws. I had hoped he was exaggerating."

Rumor had it, Jed Daltrey and his men had wintered in the Bighorn Mountain area after a botched train robbery last fall in which a cattle detective was shot dead, after singlehandedly killing several members of the gang. There was a better than good chance Jed Daltrey and his gang were lying low now at Hole-in-the-Wall.

Wyatt scrubbed his face. The plan to take Miss Cathryn to Hole-in-the-Wall was stupid and reckless. He'd have to find a safer hiding spot. But where? He knew of nowhere else they could hide out with a herd of horses. "Blackwell practically had steam coming out of his ears when I lassoed him," he said, steering the conversation away from the Daltrey Gang. "Yup. He hates my guts. Count on him being on the next train headed to Aurora."

She patted his hand. "You meant well. And you did warn me about the bad blood between you and Mr. Blackwell."

Her easy forgiveness added to his guilt. Her safety was in his hands. If she knew how often he botched up, she'd run in the opposite direction. "Trust me. Sooner or later you'll regret putting your trust in me."

"You're too fine a specimen." She winced and clapped her hand to her mouth. "Forgive me for speaking about you like a stud stallion. My mother is always chiding me about behaving like a proper lady instead of speaking and acting like a common stable hand."

"Shucks, ma'am," Wyatt drawled in exaggerated fashion, hoping to lessen her discomfort. She sure was extra pretty with her rosy cheeks. If he ever married for real, he hoped the gal would be as lovely as Miss Cathryn. "That's a mighty fine compliment."

She peeked at him quickly. "Did I mention that I'm a horse breeder?"

"Fancy that," he said impressed. "Tell me more."

She gave him a light jab with her elbow. "I don't want to bore you, or hear you say it's a man's profession."

"Nonsense. If you have the know-how, I say more power to you." Actually, he was impressed. "What qualities make for breeding good polo ponies?"

"Better than good, champion ponies," she corrected, liveliness dancing in her eyes.

"What makes a champion horse?" Pleased to have discovered her passion, he crossed his arms and closed his eyes, wanting nothing more than to spend the afternoon listening to her lilting accent.

"The first quality I—"

The door at the front of the passenger car banged open.

Wyatt reached for his revolver, but relaxed when Seth entered the passenger car with Wally close on his heels.

Garrett, Ox, and Billy called out greetings.

Ignoring them, Seth stalked up to Wyatt's bench. "Just so you know, that's the last time I'm going to step in to save your sorry neck. If it wasn't for her—" he stabbed his finger in Miss Cathryn's direction "—I might've let Blackwell shoot you."

Miss Cathryn leaned past Wyatt. "If you are going to

blame anyone, blame me. I asked for his help. He stole the ponies at my request."

Wally winked at Miss Cathryn. "Hello, beautiful."

"Mind your manners," Seth said, then turned his molten glare back on Wyatt. "You best tell everyone you cross paths with that me and Wally didn't have anything to do with stealing them horses."

"Of course," Wyatt said, feeling lower than a snake's belly.

Wally's eyes sparkled with impish delight. His bruises were turning a sickly yellowish purple. "I wanted to cover my face with a bandanna like a real train bandit, but Mr. Seth is always grouchy and ruins my fun."

Wyatt gave Wally's red bandanna a playful tug. "Seth has your best interests at heart.

Seth's glower aged his young face. "What happened with Calvin wasn't enough. Now you've dragged another innocent boy into your foolishness."

Wally's eyebrows popped. "Me? Innocent? You must be talking about some other boy."

Wyatt swallowed, but the soul-deep sickness that always accompanied memories of Calvin's broken, lifeless body refused to budge. But he wouldn't burden the others with his guilt. He offered up his knuckles to Wally. "Let's knock fists. I heard tell that's how fighters in boxing rings shake hands. I promise to be on my best behavior, if you do."

Wally grinned and his small knuckles bumped solidly into Wyatt's. "It's a deal."

"Whoa doggie, you've got some wallop in that punch,"

Wyatt said.

Wally belly-laughed, but Seth frowned. "Calvin thought you were a hoot too. Why are you still in Wyoming? Sweet Creek Ranch doesn't need more of your braggadocious antics."

The accusation knocked the wind out of Wyatt.

"Go sit down," Garrett told Seth.

"Yeah," Ox and Billy said together, not hiding their disapproval.

Seth glared back. "Mind your own business."

Wally tugged on Seth's dusty shirt. "Hey, don't go stealing my five-dollar words. Braggadocious, is my favorite standby."

Seth scowled. "Do you ever stop with the chattering?"

Wally wrinkled his nose. "You're just jealous you're not as much fun as Mr. Wyatt."

Wyatt felt horrible about making Seth's job tougher. "You best go find your seats."

"You heard 'em, kid," Seth bit out between clenched teeth. "Let's go."

The boy's shoulders sagged. "I hope everyone isn't as grouchy as you at this ranch you're taking me too."

Wyatt had been a handful when Pa Malcolm had brought him home to Sweet Creek Ranch. But between his patient lessons and Ma Viola's strict but loving hand, he settled down. His brother Ty and his ball-of-fire wife Ella ran the farm since Pa and Ma were murdered and were carrying on the mission of rescuing homeless boys. Wally was sure to fall in love with them and the ranch.

They didn't need Wyatt messing up all their hard work.

He looked Seth in the eye, man to man. "I promise to skedaddle once I'm done helping Miss Cathryn."

Seth clapped in mocking fashion. "The day can't come fast enough."

"Don't listen to him, Mr. Wyatt," Billy said, his freckled face burning bright red.

"You gotta forgive Wyatt sometime," Ox urged.

Defiance flared in Seth's eyes. "Says who?"

"He feels real bad about what happened," Garrett said.

Seth's upper lip curled. "Tell that to Calvin's grave." He grasped Wally by the arm. "Come on, kid. We got better places to be."

"I hope there's strawberry jam and bread waiting there for us," Wally said agreeably as Seth led him toward the next passenger coach.

Witnessing the wedge between Seth and the other boys deepen because of him filled every pore in Wyatt's body with regret. Most of the boys who came to the ranch settled right in, but not Seth. He remained an outsider. A loner.

One of those newfangled electric lamps everyone was raving over couldn't shine a brighter light on the truth. Sweet Creek Ranch and his family would be better off without him. And once he left Wyoming, he shouldn't look back or come back.

Chapter Twelve

An hour into the four-hour train ride to northern Wyoming, Kitty rubbed her riding boot next to her right ankle and winced. Between her throbbing ankle and the narrow wooden train bench it was impossible to get comfortable. The problem was not helped by straining to remain tight against the window to avoid contact with Haven's hard body. She'd pictured cattle rustlers as lean and desperate. Her cattle rustler would have to be built like a bank vault.

The giant black revolver on his gun belt was equally intimidating. But since almost every man in Wyoming was armed she couldn't ask him to put the weapon away. If she was going to make the West her home, she needed to get used to the sight. Better yet, she would purchase a revolver and take lessons until she mastered the art of shooting.

She flexed her foot. Her hands balled at the stab of pain and a cold sweat dampened her forehead. "Ow!"

Haven reached for her ankle. "We best take off the boot and have a look."

She batted his hand away. "It's just a sprain." If her ankle ballooned up, she would never get the boot back on.

"I'll truss you up like a Christmas goose if you fight me." The glint in his eyes was worrisome. An overgrown boy in a man's body, Haven was apt to do almost anything.

"Don't you dare." She pulled her leg up and eyed her riding boot. Clad in body-fitting breeches, she felt half naked. It was going to be impossible to remove the boot gracefully in the cramped quarters.

"Brace your back against the wall and I'll give the boot a tug," Haven said, his voice now hoarse.

He wasn't ogling her like a common lecher, but the flare of desire in his eyes was unmistakable. Her insides warmed. Flustered, she thrust her leg to the floor, crossed her ankles, and bit her lip against the sharp ache. "I'll scream if you touch me."

He chuckled and bumped her arm. "Go ahead. I'd like to hear that."

"You are not fighting fair."

"That's what you get for marrying a cattle rustler. Now give me your foot."

What had she been thinking, putting her trust in a hulk of a cowboy who joked and jested about matters large and small? And why did he have to be so handsome, with his baby blue eyes and winning smile? Expelling an annoyed breath, she swung around and thrust her boot into his lap. She extracted her revenge. "That young man Seth was not happy with you. Is he a relation of yours?"

The light fled from his eyes. "Seth is my brother."

"How many brothers do you have? You do not look a bit similar."

His smile was wistful. "We were all adopted by

Malcolm and Viola Haven."

She had struck a deeper nerve than intended, but curiosity drove her on. "Even that personable boy accompanying Seth and this Calvin you were speaking of?"

Deep sorrow marred his chiseled face. "Wally is the newest second-chance boy. I'd just as soon not speak of Cal..." His voice broke. Clearing his throat, he squeezed her foot. "You best steady yourself while I have a go at removing your boot."

She gripped the train seat and pushed back against the window as he yanked on her boot. Her heart ached for his obvious grief. "I'm sorry. I didn't mean to pry."

Haven glanced up. "That's right kind of you." He smiled, but it didn't dispel the bleakness etched in his eyes. "Did you pour glue into your boot when I wasn't looking?"

She grinned for his sake. "Don't tell me a strong cowboy like you is going to be foiled by simple footwear."

He wiggled the heel more determinedly. "Challenge accepted."

Under different circumstances, she would be totally charmed by his American brand of chivalry. "I would hate to have to cut it off. They are my favorite riding boots."

One more firm tug and her foot popped free. He lofted the boot in triumph. "Yeehaw! We done it."

Her ankle throbbing in earnest, she drew up her leg and clutched her foot. "Blimey bother, that hurts."

Haven dropped the boot, pried her hands away, and probed her ankle through her sock.

Her breath hitched. How could it hurt, but at the same

time feel good? "See, it's not broken. It's just a sprain."

His concerned gaze met hers. "Will it hold up to riding through the night and morning?"

She did not want to consider the idea of shoving her boot back on and jouncing on horseback for hours. "All night? Is that necessary?"

He nodded. "We have a head start on Blackwell, but we won't be able to travel fast with your pack of ponies. It's a good two days' ride to Hole-in-the-Wall. If that sounds too difficult, we—"

"Do not change plans on my account." She pulled her foot free, flexing it she grimaced. "A little suffering never hurt anyone."

"Ma Viola would say talk like that was plain nonsense," he said amiably, then proceeded to slip his suspenders off his broad shoulders. The rest of his words were lost on her as he tugged his shirttails free from his trousers, worked the buttons open, and drew the shirt off, leaving him naked from the waist up.

Heat rushed to her face. Mesmerized by the expanse of golden skin and toned muscle, she couldn't stop staring. "Mr. Haven, you forget yourself."

He handed her his waded-up shirt and worked on unfastening his suspenders from his trousers. "Nope, I'm Wyatt and you're Miss Cathryn."

"That is not what I meant."

The brilliance in his blue eyes deserved to be accompanied by choir of angels singing the *Hallelujah Chorus*. "I was only teasing to make you smile. Your ankle needs to be wrapped up good and tight before it swells. My shirt and suspenders ought to do the trick."

Thoroughly enjoying the spectacle, Garrett, Ox, and Billy whistled and applauded and ribbed each other.

"I'm doctoring a bad ankle, you clodhoppers," Haven said without heat. "Not putting on a show."

Deciding that checking the reactions of the other passengers would not be wise, she kneaded the white cotton shirt still warm with Haven's body heat. He didn't possess an inkling of the conceit like some blessed with physical beauty. "That is very clever of you. And kind…sacrificing your clothing for my benefit."

He shrugged, causing his pectoral muscles to flex. "This ain't nothing compared to the time I had to walk through Aurora dressed like a saloon girl. I can tell you the whole story if you like while I wrap your ankle."

Surrendering her foot, she squeezed her eyes closed. If she concentrated on his cheerful voice, all would be well. London Bridge. Who was she kidding? She was sharing a very small bench with a large half-naked man who also happened to be her *husband*. And the train carrying them was barreling northward deeper into the wilds of the American West. In less than forty-eight hours she would be taking her stolen ponies into an encampment inhabited by bank robbers and cattle rustlers.

What had happened to her safe life where tea and crumpets and polo matches were the mainstays of her days?

As her ankle was wrapped, she bit her lip against the pain. "I need your help," Haven said. "Hold the shirt in place here and here."

She sat up, and with her nose inches from a wall of solid flesh, she concentrated on the task at hand. Of course he smelled heavenly. Her mother's circle of friends turned their noises up at the odor of horse, hay, and dust, but Kitty preferred it above a garden full of flowers.

In a few quick moves, he deftly bound the shirt to her leg with the suspenders. "How's that?"

She wiggled her toes. The pressure from the makeshift wrap actually felt good. "Much better."

His smile lit up the cramped compartment.

She sucked in her breath. "Get a hold of yourself, Kitty-Girl."

"Kitty-Girl?" His drawl sounded lyrical compared to her clipped annunciation. "The name fits. May I call you Kitty-Girl instead of Miss Cathryn?"

She fanned her face. "What I wouldn't do for a spot of tea."

"I can rustle you up a drink of water." He turned to his brothers. "One of you boys got a canteen?"

Garrett, the shyest of the trio, fished his from his belongings first. "Here you go." He pulled it back at the last second. "How long you been shaving your chest, Wy?"

Haven fluttered his eyelashes in an exaggerated fashion and spoke in a girlish tone. "You're just jealous."

Ox and Billy howled with laughter.

Ox passed his coat to Haven. "Cover up before the other ladies on the train faint or fall into a tizzy."

"Amen to that," Kitty said under her breath.

But Haven rolled the coat and used it to prop up her leg.

"If you can manage a nap, you'll be glad for it later."

His kindness and genuine concern for her welfare were almost as unsettling as his lack of modesty and his ability to laugh at himself.

She closed her eyes. Sleep was impossible, but it was the only option available to put some distance between Wyatt Haven and her. Still, she couldn't say she had any desire to run back to her mother and brother and Mr. Blackwell.

Chapter Thirteen

Ten exhausting hours later, Kitty's ankle felt fine, but she was saddle sore from riding mile upon mile astride a Western saddle. Lady Winsome had sidestepped and whinnied when Haven strapped on the bulky leather monstrosity.

Worried about the extra strain of the strange saddle, she examined Winnie closely each time they had paused for a rest, but the champion pony appeared no worse for the rigors. The same could not be said for Kitty's tender backside. What she wouldn't give right now for a good English saddle!

How ungrateful did that sound?

During the brief stop in Aurora, an interesting couple called Buck and Ugly Sally had been kind enough to lend them the blanket and saddles. With the sun setting, Haven said a hasty goodbye to his brothers. They were unhappy when he insisted they continue with their plan to drive a small herd of Herefords north the next day. She was relieved he prevailed. It was bad enough that she had already dragged one innocent person into her troubles.

With Haven riding Lord Braveheart, they headed east, each leading two ponies. They were able to ride late into the night with the benefit of the nearly full moon. The road they followed quickly gave way to a beaten path stretching through an endless sea of lifeless grass and pocked with bushes called sagebrush.

Arriving at a rushing stream near midnight, they decided they had pushed themselves and the ponies enough for one day. After watering the ponies and ensuring they were properly tethered, she made her way to the crackling fire.

Squatting on his haunches next to the campfire, Haven stared at her with unabashed interest. Soup bubbled in a small kettle hanging from a tripod. Was that rosemary she smelled? The one advantage of traveling with extra horses was the ability to carry a wealth of supplies. And he appeared to be an expert at preparing food over on open fire.

"I hope you're not too tuckered to eat."

Her stomach growled. "That smells delicious."

Though the ponies couldn't have been better behaved, her arm ached from hours of clutching the lead ropes. Her leg muscles were cramping. She ought to be too exhausted to think straight, but her nerves hummed. Spending the night alone in the wilderness with a robust, handsome man was not a restful prospect. Refusing to be intimidated, she knelt on a blanket spread by the fire. "Thank you, Mr. Haven. Food would be welcome."

"You don't need to talk all formal-like for my sake." He stirred a ladle through the soup, then dished chunks of carrot, potato, and onion into a large tin mug. "We can be ourselves out here, Kitty-Girl."

Be myself? Milton lived a lie, not her. She was a horsewoman willing to risk all for her ponies. End of story. "My father called me Kitty-Girl. Now you have made me sad."

With an apologetic look, he handed her the steaming mug handle-first. "If you haven't noticed, I have a bad habit of rattling off at the mouth."

What would Herbert Cliffton, owner of a very prosperous estate, make of Wyatt Haven? Her father had believed she could do no wrong, but he could be harsh in his criticism of others. Especially the young men who came to call with the hope of courting her. It was hard to believe he had been gone for eight years. She sighed. "I prefer Kitty over Cathryn. Wyatt fits you."

Filling his mug with soup, he took a seat beside her. "My brothers call me Wy."

She spooned up the soup. "Does it taste as good as it smells?"

"Let your soup cool a bit." He stuck out his tongue and fanned his mouth. "It's hot enough to melt Beau Blackwell's mustache wax." He talked as if his mouth were stuffed with cotton.

The image of the cattle baron's droopy mustache caked with bits of wax, onion, and potato made her smile. "It's not polite to speak ill of a man one has just jilted, but that mustache is hideous."

"Like a critter crawled up on his face and died."

A fit of laughter taking hold, she held the mug at a

distance. "You're going to make me spill my soup."

Merriment danced in Wyatt's eyes. "You started it."

Hugging the warm mug to her chest, she studied the star-filled sky as a defense against his potent pull. "You clown on purpose, don't you?"

He slurped down some soup and wiped his mouth on his sleeve. "I'm always doing something foolish."

The dismissive reply didn't sit right. It was true that he was as spirited as a colt, but when he had been outgunned six to one at the train station, he took command of the situation. And at a moment's notice he had deftly arranged the many pieces of their hasty escape—stealing the ponies out from under the noses of Mr. Blackwell's men, securing last minute passage on the train, and arranging the quick marriage.

Picking up her spoon, she fished up a carrot. Wyatt was playful, but he was not dim-witted. "I don't believe you."

His laugh was infectious. "That's 'cause you don't know me."

She had smiled more in one day in his presence than she had in the last six months. "Don't change. You are perfect just as you are."

"Shucks, ma'am," he drawled in exaggerated fashion. "If you keep talking like that, you're gonna give me a swelled head."

Conceit was not one of his sins. "You still haven't answered my question. Why do you work so hard at cheering up everyone?"

He shrugged. "I never thought about it much. I suppose it's 'cause the world seems a nicer place when folks are happy."

He was continually surprising her. "I wish I had a tenth of your goodness."

Was he blushing, or was the heat from the campfire heightening the color on his cheeks? "You have a good heart."

Compared to him she'd lived a selfish, privileged life. "I cannot agree."

"I've seen you with your horses. In my experience folks who treat animals badly are likely to act that way with people."

Her heart warmed. "See, you did it again. You said just the right thing to make me feel better."

"If I'd have minded my own business, you wouldn't be here."

What would she have done if Wyatt had not been there to turn to? Would she have married Blackwell and stood by as her ponies had their tails docked? No, not even the devil could have convinced her to marry that man if he had harmed even one hair on her ponies. As for spiriting them away on her own, up against Blackwell's army of men, she would not have had a chance.

She cleared her constricted throat. "I do not know what I would have done without your gallant assistance."

He tipped his hat. "The pleasure is all mine, ma'am."

"You found today pleasant?"

The boyish twinkle in his eyes was a warning he was about to say something outrageous. "Just this time yesterday that gal Tammy was hitting me with a rhinestone studded handbag. And a fellow named Tony punched me in the nose. Whereas today, I got to steal a kiss from a pretty English girl. And I got the satisfaction of seeing the puckered-up look on Blackwell's face when we hopped on the train. So, yeah, I'd say I had a good day."

Her face heated at the mention of the stolen kiss. If she had his boldness, she would repeat his words back to him. *"The pleasure was all mine."*

He nudged her elbow, and his hard-muscled shoulder came to rest against her arm. "Eat up."

She spooned the carrot into her mouth. The spicy kick to the broth surprised. She spooned up another bite. "My, that is delicious."

"Seeing as we're married, Kitty-Girl, I can tell you my secret ingredient. Cayenne pepper."

"It almost burns." She sipped another spoonful of broth. "It also makes me hungry for more." Wyatt had the same effect on her. Hearing him call her Kitty-Girl and reference their marriage was not as troubling as mere moments before. And then there was the lovely toe-tingling kiss.

Her insides warmed, recalling the wonderful sensation of his wide, firm mouth moving over hers. If he tried to steal another kiss what would she do?

She could kiss him back. Just to see how it felt. Would the kiss taste deliciously spicy? The notion was shocking. And exciting.

The ponies stirred and whinnied.

Wyatt set aside his mug and scrambled to his feet with his revolver drawn.

Kitty stood and searched the dark for danger.

"Stay here while I have a look around." He strode toward the stream.

She hurried to the ponies. Dancing at the end of their leads, they greeted her with nervous nickers. "Hush, Winnie," she whispered and patted the chestnut snout sniffing at her shawl.

The other ponies reached their noses toward her, wanting their share of affection and reassurance. She bathed attention on each while scanning the shadows of the surrounding sagebrush.

A sharp cry pierced the air.

She cringed, dropped to all fours, and groped for a rock or stick to act as a suitable weapon.

Eyes wide with fright, the ponies once again fought to get free of their tethers.

"Steady now," she called. Her fingers found a sharp-edged stone. She grasped the stone and, standing, she held it at the ready. "Steady now."

All but Duchess Lovey were *made ponies*. The years of training and experience on the polo field showed as they settled at the familiar command. Only Duchess Lovey continued to struggle.

A dark figure zigzagged through the shadows.

She lofted the stone higher. As with Duchess Lovey, her instincts were shouting at her to run. If she moved fast, she could probably save herself and Lady Winsome. She stood her ground.

"Kitty-Girl, it's me, Wyatt."

She whirled.

Wreathed in a halo of moonlight, he strode toward her.

"You can put that rock down. It was just a she-cat taking a drink from the stream."

"A cat?" she gasped. "You grow them big in Wyoming."

"A mountain lion," he clarified, stopping a hair's breadth away.

Lady Winsome and Lord Braveheart brushed against him in a welcoming manner.

The thought of a mountain lion attacking her ponies raised the hairs on her neck. "Why didn't you shoot it?"

Wyatt pried the rock from her hand. "I caught sight of her as she disappeared into the brush. But you don't have to worry, she won't be back. Mountain lions are more afraid of us than we are them."

Tell that to her quaking legs and arms. "I hate you for looking so calm."

He chuckled and offered her his elbow. "If anyone should be peeved, it's me. Why didn't you stay by the fire, like I told you?"

"Would you if your brothers were in danger?"

"No, ma'am. I guess I would do the same as—"

"Don't shoot." A boy burst from the brush, tripping over his feet he landed face first in the dirt. He picked himself up, and looking over his shoulder, he ran headlong into Wyatt.

"Whoa up." Wyatt caught the boy under the arms saving him from falling again.

The boy continued to stare into the dark. "Did you see that mountain lion? I thought I was a goner."

Wyatt gaped as he dusted off the boy. "Wally, what are

you doing out here?"

She was as shocked as Wyatt. "Are you alone? Where's your horse? I would hate for it to fall prey to the mountain lion."

Wally hiked up the too big breeches floating about his waist. "He's tied up on the other side of the stream. I'm riding Mr. Wyatt's horse."

"You stole my horse?" Wyatt searched behind himself quickly. Then glared down at Wally. "Where's Seth?"

"I gave him the slip." Wally dismissed his bragging with a flap of the hand. "And I didn't steal your horse. That big fellow named Ox saddled Charger for me."

"Seth and Ox meant for you to ride to Sweet Creek Ranch," Wyatt said in exasperation.

Wally poked out his bottom lip. "Why would I want to go live on a boring ranch when I could go to Hole-in-the-Wall with you?"

Wyatt's teeth ground together so tightly, she thought she heard his jaw crack. "No. Absolutely not. I will not take you within fifty miles of that den of sin."

Wally turned to her. "I promise to be good. You can whack me in the head if I mess up."

The hopefulness in eyes broke her heart. The moonlight magnified the mottled bruises covering his face. Wyatt had told her the whole sad story of Seth shooting Wally's father upon catching him in a drunken rage beating his son with a shovel. How could she say yes and expose Wally to more danger? But sending him back without supervision was out of the question.

Lady Winsome jostled her arm. Kitty hugged Winnie

around the neck. Why was she wavering? Putting the well-being of a child over her ponies was the obvious choice. How easy it had been to call Milton wicked and selfish. Apparently it was a family trait.

Releasing her hold on the pony, she knelt in front of Wally and held his cold hands. "Are you hungry? Mr. Wyatt made some delicious soup."

Wally gave her a peck on the cheek. "I thought you'd never ask, beautiful."

She glanced up at Wyatt. "Once he's safe at Sweet Creek Ranch, we can decide where to go from there."

"Hey," Wally complained. "That wasn't part of the deal."

Wyatt frowned. "You and I are gonna have a nice long talk on proper manners while you help me retrieve my horse."

Wally sighed. "Mr. Wyatt, you were supposed to be more fun than Seth."

Wyatt helped her stand. Looking as conflicted as she felt, he squeezed her hand. "I'm sorry. I understand how much those horses mean to you."

He did understand. Wyatt Haven was a good man. A very good man. Why did that make her want to cry? She straightened her shoulders. "If a ten-year-old boy could track us that easily, I suppose Mr. Blackwell would have soon caught up with us."

"But riding a posse into Sweet Creek Ranch won't give him second thoughts like riding one into Hole-in-the-Wall would have."

A shiver went through her. "A posse? That sounds

ominous."

"If you mean someone could get hurt, you got that right."

She would never forgive herself if Wyatt or his family suffered injury or worse. She dug her nails into her palms. "I regret asking for your help. It was wrong and self-centered."

"Whoa up," he said. "Give me a moment." His hands resting on the gun belt slung low across his hips and his white cowboy hat shadowing eyes, he stared into the distance, appearing thoroughly capable of causing his own mayhem.

She moved closer, drawn to his powerful presence. "What are you thinking?"

His gaze met hers. "I want to continue to Hole-in-the-Wall."

"What about Wally?" she asked, remaining torn.

The boy's eyes lit with hope. "I can take care of myself."

Wyatt hitched his thumb over his shoulder. "Go get yourself some grub."

"Something sure smells scrumptious." Wally scurried toward the campfire.

Wyatt offered her a reassuring look. "Boys grow up fast in the high country. Cowboy work ain't for the timid. And it'll be best for my family if we keep to our plan. Seth is most likely hot on Wally's trail. He'll take the boy off our hands in short order. Until then, I'll just need to keep him and you and your horses safe."

She had never met a man quite like Wyatt. He was

stating facts, not bragging or expecting her to follow orders. It was a good bet his brothers were cut from the same cloth. "Thank you. I will sleep better now we have talked this out."

He unleashed one of his gorgeous smiles. "Liar."

She smiled in return. "Horse hooey sound better. Liar is so harsh."

"Horse hooey? And here I thought you used only big fancy words."

"Hooey isn't fancy enough for you?"

His warm laugh was a pleasurable reward. "Blimey bother wasn't very dignified. But I like the way you sound when you talk."

"I said that aloud?"

He grinned. "When I was working on your ankle."

She had never been one for flirting or playful banter, but with Wyatt it came naturally. And it was infinitely preferable to dwelling on the trouble chasing after them and the danger waiting ahead.

Chapter Fourteen

Wyatt enjoyed spicing up life with a dash of excitement, but the last twenty-four hours had set a record even by his daredevil standards. He married an English heiress. Stole six polo ponies from a cattle baron. And inherited responsibility for a wisecracking boy by the name of Wally.

As impressive as this feat was, yesterday's extraordinary adventures appeared tame compared to his grand plan to waltz unannounced into an outlaw camp. Bank robbers and cattle rustlers weren't what you'd call neighborly. Any welcome they rolled out would involve cussing and revolvers and shotguns.

The noontime sun blazed high over the red sandstone cliffs as the horses negotiated the steep rocky pass appropriately called Hole-in-the-Wall. Towering mesa walls stretched for fifty miles, this gap providing the only passage to the valley beyond. If there was a lookout stationed on the plateau above, which was guaranteed if Jed Daltrey was around, their presence had been noted a long time ago.

Wyatt was plenty pleased over reuniting with his horse. Kitty's ponies were excellent animals, Lord Braveheart being one of the fastest, strongest horses he'd had the privilege to ride, but he wasn't Charger. And this was no Sunday picnic. If trouble broke out, he didn't want to guess at his horse's abilities.

Cresting the trail, Wyatt encouraged Charger forward.

Just like when he was a wide-eyed fourteen-year-old orphan who'd been befriended by a veteran cattle rustler and was herding his first batch of stolen cattle to this remote outpost, he was in awe of Hole-in-the-Wall's lavish landscape. Cattle grazed on the grassy plateau, overlooking a canyon land dotted with giant boulders and chiseled buttes. Tenacious cottonwoods hugged the banks of a meandering steam, the perfect spot to soak your feet or soak a fishing line.

"Wow, there are cabins and horse pens and barns," Wally said, voice plum full of eagerness, as he trotted along on Lord Braveheart.

Wyatt couldn't share his enthusiasm. The presence of the cattle meant a rustling outfit was present.

Kitty drew up beside him.

He held his breath as she surveyed the six dilapidated cabins used as a winter hideout for desperados of every stripe.

She was the picture of beauty. Surrounded by her ponies beneath the wide blue expanse of Wyoming sky, seating her horse in fine style, her back straight and her head held high. "This would be a wonderful spot for a polo pony ranch."

"Impossible." The unexpected comment tickled his funny bone. "You couldn't want to live way out here with no society for company or stores for shopping."

She smiled in return. "Ask my brother Milton or my mother, and they would tell you I would be quite happy to never attend another garden party or ball and that I could not care less if my clothing were three seasons out of fashion."

"Hoo wee, you're something else. That explains why I want to call you Kitty-Girl."

A hint of pink colored her cheeks. "Does it?"

Underneath her fancy top hat and la-di-da riding outfit, she was a gal who loved horses. That was real. That was something he could get his arms around. The memory of holding her and kissing the daylights out of her arose. Hoo wee, that had been real nice.

"Mr. Wyatt, we got company." Wally was pointing at the dozen armed men filing out of the largest cabin. "Yes!" The boy pumped his fist. "They're wearing blue bandannas. I can tell everyone I hid out with the Daltrey Gang."

Wyatt shifted in the saddle and banished thoughts of kissing. Keeping Kitty and Wally safe was his top priority. He'd need all his wits to come out unscathed by a run-in with Jed Daltrey and his gang. "Don't get too excited, kid. You ain't seen the inside of those cabins. They're not exactly cheerful. Unless you're fond of bedbugs."

Kitty blanched. "Bedbugs?"

"There's no reason to get discombobulated over a few

115

measly bedbugs," Wally said, affably. "Now if it's lice, that's a diff—"

"Button it, kid," Wyatt said, but his annoyance was directed inward. He turned an apologetic look on Kitty. "I was thinking only of the danger. I should've warned you about the less than pleasant living conditions."

Her features composed once more, she touched a hand to her thick brown hair. "A little itching and scratching never hurt anybody."

Wyatt had always assumed society women were more excitable than a hen house full of squawking chickens. But Kitty continued to surprise him. Yes siree, determination and grit were mighty handsome on a woman. "But you'd rather be bunking under the stars."

A hint of a smile curved her lips. "You read my mind."

No, but he wished he could.

"I get to claim any bed I want," Wally boasted.

Wyatt had all he could do not to strangle the lead ropes clasped in his left hand. His other hand was perched on his hip, within reaching distance of his Colt .45. "Don't do anything foolish."

Wally wrinkled his pug nose. "You need to work on being more trustful."

"You probably said the same thing to Seth, right before you ran off."

The rascal grinned. "How did you know?"

The boy was too charming for his own good. "You remind me of myself, kid. That's how."

"Holy moly, I never seen so many guns," Wally said as their horses closed on the collection of cabins and men.

116

"Steady, Winnie." Kitty stroked the filly's neck.

A jolt of energy rocketed through Wyatt as Jed Daltrey's face came into focus. They went way back, him and Jed did. Joined a notorious cattle rustling outfit a short time apart and immediately started jostling to win the favor of the outfit boss, Red Calder, who encouraged their worst impulses. Not a healthy recipe for two boys in a hurry to become men, believing carousing in saloons and devil-may-care adventures made them grown up. What it made them was extra stupid.

"Wait here with Wally," he instructed Kitty, passing over the ponies' leads. He shared a man-to-man look with Wally. "Help Miss Cathryn with steadying the horses. She won't be happy with us if anything happens to them."

Jed met him halfway. Years of reckless living usually took a toll, but the tanned wrinkles edging Jed's green eyes and the white scar punctuating his pointed chin conveyed a roguishness that was the envy of other men. If Wyatt was a girl, he'd be swooning over Jed Daltrey.

Wyatt brought Charger to a stop, and leaned casual-like on his saddle horn. "Howdy, Jed. How you been?"

Jed's chapped lips curved with a tight smile. "I weren't expecting such a friendly-like greeting, on account my gang busted up Garrett's face and done burned his barn to the ground."

Wyatt knew what Pa Malcolm and Ma Viola would have said. "Revenge is the Lord's business. Not mine."

A deep laugh you could listen to all day long rolled out of Jed. "That's not exactly the song you were singing that time I winged you by accident with my shotgun."

"Accident, my foot." Wyatt rubbed the walnut-size gouge on the underside of his arm. The doctor who patched him up told him if the bullet had hit an inch higher he'd have a gimpy arm. "I wanted you to peel the leech off my arm. Not blast it with your gun."

"Next time, don't yell, '*Shoot, Shoot.*'"

"A leech sucking you dry of blood has a way of rattling a body," Wyatt said in his defense.

Jed grinned. "You sure were surprised."

Wyatt had always had a difficult time staying angry with Jed. Back then, the outlaw hadn't been malicious. No, he and Wyatt shared the tendency to act before thinking. The difference was Wyatt would feel bad and promise to do better whereas Jed never apologized.

"Next time I'm shooting back." Wyatt used a grave tone that sounded strange to his ear.

Jed shrugged. "Fair enough." He leaned to the side and studied Kitty and Wally with undisguised curiosity. "Not likely you brang them to Hole-in-the-Wall by… *accident*."

The half-dozen men wearing blue bandannas were creeping forward, reminding Wyatt of a pack of mangy wolves eager to make a kill.

He straightened and planted his hands on his gun belt. "We're just passing through. Got us some stolen horses. There's a good chance a posse will come looking for us."

"The ponies are mine by right," Kitty called out.

Wyatt glanced back. This was no time to explain. Allowing Jed and his men to believe they were lawbreakers wanting to hide out at Hole-in-the-Wall was a gamble. But a good one. Past expedience told him there was a measure of camaraderie among thieves. "I got everything under control here," he said in an agreeable tone.

She was an isle of calm amid her ponies' nervous prancing and Wally's wide-eyed gawking. She considered his request for a long moment, then gave a slight nod of her head.

Ridiculously happy over her trusting him, he turned his attention back to Jed. He saw no reason to mention Beau Blackwell would be leading the posse. "We're just looking to stay a few days before moving on."

Amusement shone in Jed's green eyes. "I were right about you. I knew outlawing had got in your blood. I told that do-gooder Malcolm Haven you'd eventually get bored on the straight and narrow and come slinking back to us sinners."

Wyatt smiled back despite the sick feeling in the pit of his stomach. He couldn't deny the rush of exhilaration provoked by the dash into Hole-in-the-Wall. This valley had been his home for two winters. He'd be lying if he said he'd hated it. And leaving the outlaw life wasn't his idea. If Pa Malcolm and Ma Viola hadn't rescued him, like as not he'd be known as one of Red Calder's boys, instead of being counted among the Havens' second-chance boys.

Yep, he should avoid this place like a stampede of Texas Longhorns, but presently there was no help for it. "Well, Jed," he drawled, "that would be the second time in your life you've been right. The first would be when you looked in a mirror and realized how ugly you are."

The men hooted at the insult. Jed just grinned. "I have

a bottle of whiskey if you'd care to share a glass or two."

With the immediate possibility of getting shot or run off behind them, it could only help to continue in this friendly vein. Plus, Wyatt liked nothing better than to sit late into the night spouting tall tales and indulging in harmless banter. Why, in no time at all, the outlaw crew would be pudding in his hand.

Kitty and Wally moved forward, flanking him.

Reminded of his duty, he tipped his Stetson. "Thank you for the kind invite, but I'm more of a root beer kind of guy."

More laughter ensued.

"Your sweetheart don't look pleased," one of the men yelled.

"Boss, you been complaining about the cold," someone else called out. "Invite the little lady to warm you up."

A slew of lewd suggestions peppered the air.

Kitty paled.

"Shut your traps," Wyatt warned.

Meanwhile, Jed ogled Kitty like a buck in rut. "Dump this fool, sugar. And I promise to give you a real good time."

"I highly doubt that," Kitty replied, her clipped British accent a rebuke all by itself.

Jed sauntered closer. "You got spunk, I'll give you that."

His blood ready to explode out the top of his head, Wyatt had never felt this protective. "Miss Cathryn is my wife. The next man that forgets it will answer to my fists."

"Hey, I was gonna marry her," Wally exclaimed, face

puckering. "I wouldn't have gotten my hopes up if I knew you was a married couple."

The assembled men whooped and laughed at that.

Jed chuckled as well. "You don't need to pretend to be married for my sake. I don't touch a gal unless I've been invited to or I've paid for the privilege." He looked over his shoulder at his men. "I'll shoot anyone who speaks crude to the nice lady. Now git back to your own business."

The men dispersed with little grumbling. Jed saluted Wyatt. "Let me know if you need any help setting up." He headed back to his cabin, whistling through his teeth like Red used to.

Kitty exhaled loudly. "That went more smoothly than I expected."

Yes, too smooth. Jed Daltrey wanted something from Wyatt. But what?

Chapter Fifteen

Fat raindrops splattered the ground. After spending hours riding the ridge as the official lookout, Wyatt was soaked to the bone. All remained quiet around the cabins in the valley below. Kitty's ponies were safe behind the rails of a small corral. The first night in the outlaw camp had passed without incident. He scanned the empty miles of scrub brush they'd crossed yesterday, but still saw no sign of a posse.

Would Blackwell make the long ride to Hole-the-Wall based on only a hunch? The dark clouds hanging over the valley didn't look to be going anywhere. A heavy rain would help erase their tracks. The rumors his brothers agreed to spread, that Kitty and Wyatt were headed to California and Chicago and Canada might help, especially as word of their hasty marriage became public knowledge.

If Blackwell had an expert tracker who did manage to pick up their trail, he and his posse would be riding up the Hole-in-the-Wall pass before long. Even so, that would give him and Kitty a good two to three hours head start to outrun them to the Rosewood Ranch. If they left behind four of the six ponies, and he rode Charger and she rode Lady Winsome, they would have a decent chance of escaping.

That was a lot of ifs. And that plan didn't factor in Wally.

They couldn't go anywhere until Seth arrived.

And Seth was coming, of that Wyatt had no doubt. First, his tracking abilities may not be on par with a bloodhound, but he was plenty good. That aside, Seth was sharp-minded enough to have guessed at Wally's intentions and undoubtedly was placing all the blame on Wyatt for acting all friendly and smiling and joking with the boy. What else could Wyatt have done? He'd never snarled or glowered at folks and wasn't likely to start at it this late in life.

The foul weather was slowing Seth down, but he was coming. The only question was, would he try to bust Wyatt's nose when he arrived?

The men scheduled to relieve him of the watch rode up the ridge, the rain pelting their beat-up black Stetsons and boot-length duster jackets.

Several hours later, after catching up on some sleep, Wyatt trudged through the mud to the big cabin occupied by Jed Daltrey and his gang to round up Wally.

More concerned than angry that the boy had disobeyed his order to avoid the outlaw gang, he ducked inside the cabin and halted, reluctant to go any farther. A puddle quickly formed around his boots.

Cigar smoke blanketed the dank room. The smell of sweat mingled with the reek of wet socks. The men circling a rickety oak table barely glanced up from their poker game. Jed sat in front of a pot-bellied stove, his feet propped on a log waiting to be tossed in the fire. Wally's short legs were stretched in a copycat pose beside the outlaw.

Jed nodded to an empty chair next to the stove. "Sit a spell. The coffee is drinkable, and the fire is blazing hot."

The offer was tempting. But Wyatt had promised Kitty he'd be right back to eat the stew she'd prepared. She was right proud of her first attempt to cook a meal. He didn't have the heart to tell her calling the pot of scorched mush stew was criminal.

"Come along," he instructed Wally.

The boy crossed his ankles. "Jed says I can sleep here if I want. Tell Miss Cathryn goodnight for me."

Wyatt scrubbed his face. The boy wasn't a prisoner. He couldn't be forced to do anything. Even if it was in his best interest.

The smug smile on Jed's face proved he appreciated Wyatt's predicament. "We got extra bunks."

"He don't need your kind of trouble," Wyatt said, and yes, he was snarling. Returning his focus to Wally, he resorted to bribery. "You sure? I got some humdinger stories from my days in Texas I planned to share with you and Miss Cathryn."

Wally held up a light blue bandanna. "Jed asked me to join his gang."

Wyatt stalked to the stove, sat on the edge of a grimy wooden chair, and peered into Wally's expectant eyes. "Cattle rustling and train robbing are dangerous."

124

Wally shrugged. "It would be more exciting than ranch work. Jed told me about all the fun you had together when you worked for a fellow called Red Calder."

Jed held out a silver bullet on the palm of his hand. "Remember all the crowing we done when Red gave us each one of these after our first-time rustling cattle?"

Wyatt had grinned for a week. He kept the silver bullet in the burlap sack with his other mementos. But he wouldn't give Jed the satisfaction of knowing that little fact.

Wyatt hadn't been much older than Wally when he became one of Red Calder's boys. Those shouldn't have been happy days, but it turned out Wyatt was good at cattle rustling. Real good. And Red knew how to brag on a boy. Wyatt would walk around feeling ten feet tall after a successful raid.

Of course, getting shot full of holes wasn't fun. Yep, now Wyatt was glowering at Jed. "Red left me for dead after the Powder River showdown."

Jed dropped the silver bullet back in his shirt pocket. "Red never could figure out how you outsmarted the Grim Reaper."

Getting shot turned out to be the best thing to ever happen to Wyatt. He liked to think he would have given up his outlaw ways if he hadn't taken those bullets. Then again Jed hadn't.

Wally was staring wide-eyed. He needed to be convinced in a hurry Jed didn't have his best interests in mind.

Wyatt snagged the blue cloth square from Wally's

hand. "Did Jed tell you he lost three men last fall? He made the mistake of robbing a train carrying a delegation of cattle detectives."

The poker game ground to a halt.

"Don't talk disrespectful about the dead," one of the card players warned.

"Jed wasn't at fault," said the man sitting across the table.

The first man nodded. "There was only supposed to be one lawman on the train. Not a whole passel of 'em."

Red Calder's men had been equally loyal.

Jed exhaled heavily. "I'm looking to rebuild my crew."

"And you're starting with a ten-year-old?" Wyatt asked, angry with himself for feeling any sympathy for the man who had knocked out Garrett and burned his barn.

Jed narrowed his eyes at Wally. "You told me you were twelve."

The boy hopped off his chair. "It's not my fault you believed me."

Wyatt tossed aside the bandanna.

Jed hitched his thumb toward the door. "Get going, kid. Come back when you're older and—"

The front door banged open and one of watchmen escorted Seth inside.

Seth crossed the room with a few long strides, his dark eyes fixed on Wyatt. "You'll never guess what's happened, Wy."

Wyatt stared flabbergasted. His other brothers called him Wy, but not Seth. "I hope it's good news."

Seth removed his soaked Stetson and flashed a rare

smile. "Blackwell's heart gave out while he was organizing the posse."

Wyatt's jaw went slack. "Blackwell is dead?"

Seth casually scanned his surroundings. "No, but Doc Craig said it don't look good."

Kitty needed to be told. Blackwell's resting at death's door changed everything.

Chapter Sixteen

In the wake of learning Beau Blackwell might die, the cloying, musty air filling the one-room cabin made it impossible for Kitty to breathe. She couldn't think straight with Wyatt towering over her, concern for her feelings filling his eyes.

She bolted for the door, rushed outside, and hurried to the rickety corral where her ponies were penned. The rain had ceased, and the rays of sun assaulted the thinning clouds. Seeking her attention, Lady Winsome and the others stretched their necks over the decaying rails.

Aghast at the possibility her actions might be responsible for a man's death, she blindly stroked their noses.

Wyatt strode to her side. "Don't blame yourself. Beau Blackwell never lived a quiet day in his life. His anger over you jilting him isn't the first time he's been spitting mad. If anyone can swear to that, I can."

The news about Blackwell was as dizzying as when she and Milton were children somersaulting down the steep grassy knoll at their Somerset country estate. Mother,

Father, and the gardener watched with indulgent smiles as they ran up the hillock to experience the thrill again, but the fun ended abruptly when Kitty cracked her head on a rock. She had been more frightened than hurt, but that was the last time she cared to tumble topsy-turvy down hills.

She clutched her trembling hands. "He has a daughter. And employees." She did not know Caroline Blackwell, but she understood the grief of losing a father. And despite Beau Blackwell's many faults, the housemaid Consuela and ranch foreman Amos Little seemed loyal to him.

Wyatt made of the horses for a moment even as his eyes remained on her. "He might pull through. Doc Craig will take real good care of him."

Her legs weak, she turned and leaned against the corral rails. She stabbed at a stray tear. Tears, truly? But she never ever cried. "Running away was so unlike me."

"I wouldn't know about that." Wyatt's voice was as gentle as summer breeze. "But I can see you have a good heart."

She wanted to believe him, but was afraid if she gazed into a mirror she would not recognize the person staring back. "What comes next?" she whispered. "I don't know what comes next."

Wyatt rested his elbows on the top rail so his powerful shoulder pressed against her shoulder. "We'll leave for Rosewood Ranch first thing tomorrow. You'll feel more like yourself among friends."

The red sandstone cliffs and miles of barren sagebrush stretching into the distance could not be more different from London. If Milton hadn't stolen the snuffbox, she would likely be married to a scion of the British polo world. That was where she felt at home. Wasn't it? Not out here in this yawning wilderness. "I will hold you to that promise."

Wyatt ducked his head and kicked at the dirt. "Not all the cattle barons are as cold-hearted as Blackwell. Your brother will find you a nicer fellow for you to marry."

That was depressing. But what was her other choice? Going back to London was not an option. To receive her inheritance, she must marry. From what she had seen, Wyoming high country couldn't be more perfect for establishing a polo pony estate. But finding the right husband?

She glanced at Wyatt. They were legally wed. No, she couldn't. Could she?

Pure cowboy from his wide-brimmed hat to his battered leather gun belt, to his pointed boots and silver spurs, he was untamed, wild-blooded, and dangerously daring.

Heat rushed through her.

Winnie forced her head between them.

Thank goodness. A good dose of horse sense was just what was called for.

Laughing as though he'd read her mind, Wyatt pushed away from the fence. "I'll go let Jed know we'll leave in the morning."

Unsettled by her fascination with his rolling gait as he walked away, she curved her arm under Winnie's neck and pressed her face to the mare's soft cheek.

Running away had nothing to do with wanting to escape the British landed gentry set or societal expectations or her father's dreams for her.

No.

The marriage of convenience to a cowboy, fleeing to the whimsically named Hole-in-the-Wall, going to Henrietta's Rosewood Ranch, and her entire life revolved around one focus.

Her ponies.

They were her happiness, her comfort, her reason for getting out of bed each day.

Nothing else mattered.

Chapter Seventeen

The next morning Wyatt and Seth lined the horses along a flimsy hitching post preparing for their departure from Hole-in-the-Wall. Jed Daltrey stood outside the main cabin with his arms crossed and watched in silence. Wally sat slumped on the stairs grousing that he was plenty old enough to be a train robber. He mixed in the occasional complaint that nobody was listening to him or cared what he wanted. Kitty remained inside the small one-room cabin, taking advantage of the privacy to freshen her clothes and hair. Done saddling Charger, Wyatt lifted the collar of his buckskin jacket to protect his neck from the morning chill. Spring was his favorite time of the year. Sunny days, bursting with the life and vitality that vanquished the remnants of winter. But he couldn't shake the sense of doom and guilt dogging his heels since learning of Beau Blackwell's critical condition.

Much as he disliked Blackwell, he didn't want to see the man die. Even if it would make life easier for his family and the business interests of Sweet Creek Ranch. Would he feel differently if his action weren't partly responsible for Blackwell's heart giving out? Such morbid thoughts weren't helping his mood any.

Jed moseyed over. "If you change your mind about joining my gang, I'll be glad—"

"Nope." Wyatt shook his head. "Not that I don't appreciate the offer."

Jed turned his snake-green eyes on Seth. "That's a fine pair of Schofields you're carrying. Nobody appreciates the talents of a young gunfighter like I do."

Seth finished fastening the bridle on Wally's mount and glared at Wyatt. "Should I tell Garrett you and Jed Daltrey are best buddies?"

The sarcasm stung. "Beat it, Jed," Wyatt said.

"Don't be surprised if you come to regret your decision." Jed strolled off whistling through his teeth.

Seth gave Wyatt a companionable slap on the back. "Right. That will be our secret."

Wyatt couldn't help wondering if an impostor had replaced the perpetually sour-faced Seth. "You're not usually so agreeable in the morning."

Seth hooked his thumbs in his gun belt. "Why shouldn't I be in a stinking pleasant mood? If your stupidity was gonna kill someone else, it couldn't happen to a nicer fella than Blackwell. Even if he don't croak, there's no way you can stay in Wyoming now that you branded yourself as a horse thief."

Wyatt's gut clenched. Seth's deepening bitterness and hate killed him, knowing full well he was responsible for this latest dive. The further Seth continued down this path the less the chance of his ever being settled or happy.

Wyatt didn't know how to fix matters. Seth had made it plenty clear he didn't want apologies or lectures, especially not from him.

He pretended to check Charger's saddle belt. "You don't have to worry about me staying in Wyoming. I'll giddy up out of here once I'm done assisting Miss Cathryn."

"Who said I was worried?" Seth shot back.

They both stopped and stared as Kitty stepped out of the cabin. The elegance of her up-swept hair, freshly brushed riding outfit put the outlaw camp to shame.

"Try not to get Beau Blackwell's bride killed while you're *helping* her," Seth said, shattering the silence. "Not that I care, but her family might."

The thought of harm befalling Kitty hollowed out Wyatt. "I care." She'd proved she was tough as nails underneath the pretty sheen. Her horsemanship was unparalleled. If she'd been trained to use a gun, he didn't doubt she could take care of herself as well as any lone rider traveling through the wilderness.

Seth dragged his Schofield from his gun belt, cracked open the six-shooter, and inspected the chamber. "That won't help her when you pull another rash stunt."

The five days since Wyatt had made Kitty's acquaintance had gone by in a flash. He'd be lying to say he was looking forward to going separate ways. He'd miss her pretty perfume. Her refined accented voice. Her lovely lips curving with a smile in response to his teasing.

"Don't tell me you're sweet on her?" Seth's smirk was lethal. "A classy lady like her wouldn't give a two-bit cattle rustler a second thought."

"You can stop beating me over the head with the truth," Wyatt growled. "Once I deliver Miss Cathryn to Rosewood Ranch, I'll head out of the state quicker than you can say yeehaw."

"Yeehaw!" Seth crowed. Holstering his Schofield, he jabbed his elbow into Wyatt's side. "Don't look so sad. You'll bounce back just fine wherever you land, smiling and joking and generally acting like a fool. You'll soon have whole pack of new friends."

"Yeehaw," Wyatt repeated blindly.

It didn't matter if he was right fond of his old friends and days spent helping Ty and Ella run Sweet Creek Ranch. Moving on to the nomadic life in a Wild West show was the right thing to do. He'd learn to love it. Even if it killed him.

Chapter Eighteen

With the outlaw camp several hours behind them, Kitty gloried in guiding Lady Winsome beside a rushing stream. A creek, as Wyatt called it. The Americanism suited the beautifully severe landscape and the gash of muddy water snaking through the bottom land.

She had yet to tire of watching the swell of the spring run-off eat away at the dirt banks. If only this time could go on forever. The shifting of the saddle under her. The leather reins chafing calluses. The day spent enveloped in a wonderful horsey smell. Pure perfection.

Between the long sea voyage and cross-country journey by train, weeks and weeks had passed since she had been able to enjoy these simple pleasures she found so very vital. Her ponies had weathered the prolonged hardship well and remained as hearty and healthy as could be hoped.

The days ahead held the promise of more uncertainty. This brief time of rejuvenation was beyond lovely.

Wyatt slowed his handsome horse and studied her for a long moment. "You been mighty quiet, Kitty-Girl."

She lifted her face to the sun. "I like the peacefulness of this place."

"It's safe to guess you're not missing Wally's nonstop squawking over his rights being ignored."

They hadn't traveled quite three miles from Hole-in-the-Wall when Seth and Wally parted ways with them on an eastward track.

Questions surrounding Wyatt swirled through her mind. How had such a good man become a cattle rustler? Why had he riled a cattle baron to help a stranger? Why did Seth wear his anger toward Wyatt like a badge?

Curiosity finally won the war with proper comportment. "Seth is rather displeased with you."

Wyatt clenched his chiseled jaw and stared straight ahead. "We lost a second-chance boy. I was to blame."

Garrett, Ox, and Billy hadn't been angry with Wyatt. "Second-chance boy?" she asked. He had used the term on the train when he was wrapping her ankle.

Wyatt exhaled heavily. "That's what we call the boys we rescue. Sweet Creek Ranch isn't only a cattle ranch, it a place for boys who have been orphaned or homeless. Garrett, Ox, Seth, me, we were all second-chance boys."

The nobleness of this man and his family awed her. "It sounds like a special place.

His blue eyes met hers. "The best in the world. And I failed that trust."

Her heart ached for his deep grief and guilt. "Surely whatever happened was an accident."

The silence stretched on for a long time. Wyatt cleared his throat. "Little Calvin was only seven. Seth found the boy picking through the trash behind a Texas whorehouse. His ma had abandoned him and lit out to California with a wanted murderer. Calvin moped about Sweet Creek, missing his ma and crying himself to sleep every night."

Kitty stroked Winnie to comfort herself, and in lieu of offering similar ease to Wyatt. "That poor child."

Wyatt gave a small nod. "I was hoping to cheer up Calvin by showing off my trick riding skills. Calvin loved horses. The only time he smiled was when I took him to visit the horse barn and pastures. He was particularly obsessed with a white stallion that was new to the ranch. I warned Calvin to stay clear of White Diamond. The whole family was gathered around me and Charger, impressed with my new trick of galloping on Charger blindfolded."

"Were you blindfolded or was Charger?" she interrupted, unable to help herself.

Wyatt actually smiled. "Me, of course. I would never intentionally put Charger in danger."

Her fascination with him grew. "And you taught yourself to do this because..."

He shifted in his saddle. "I thought riding in a Wild West show sounded like a good time."

"So, you did not plan to remain at Sweet Creek Ranch?"

"I'm not one for making plans, Kitty-Girl." The light went out of his eyes. "You've seen for yourself there's not a lot of sense behind most of what I do."

"Did Calvin fall from a horse and die while trying to copy your tricks?"

Swirling heat ruffled the fringe of his buckskin jacket.

"Calvin climbed on White Diamond bareback when no one was looking and kicked the horse into a gallop. He'd worked himself to a kneeling position when the horse made a hard-right cut near the old well."

Kitty squeezed her eyes shut. She didn't need to hear more. "I am so sorry, Wyatt. I do not know what to say."

"There's no words to make the matter better. And Seth has every right in the world to hold what happened to little Calvin against me."

Wyatt's guilt-ridden conscience was part and parcel of the tragedy. Yes, he was audacious and impetuous, and a bit wild, but he was not irresponsible. From all she had seen, he was a man of his word. Protective of his loved ones and friends. He put others' needs before his own. "You should not blame yourself. It was an accident. The boy's mother failed little Calvin. Not you."

Wyatt stared into the distance. "That's what my other brothers say."

She had only met a few of his brothers, but Wyatt's affection and close ties to his large family was impossible to miss. She and Milton had always been rivals, with her as Father's favorite and Milton as Mother's. A few short days ago she would not have believed that an orphan and cattle rustler would know more about happiness, love, and affection than she did.

She searched for a means to comfort Wyatt, but if he couldn't accept his brothers' words she doubted anything she said would help.

Charger and Winnie brushed close together. She and Wyatt rode in silence for hours.

Chapter Nineteen

After baking in the sun for hours, Kitty was grateful when Wyatt announced they would stop for the night beside a series of short waterfalls. The ledge of rock dipping down to a shallow pool looked inviting.

Hobbling the horses, they left them to graze on the tufts of grass sprouting in abundance. And made their way back to the neat mound of supplies. Wool blankets, blackened cookpots, bags filled with potatoes, onions, and coffee beans, canned kidney beans and corn, and saddles draped with Wyatt's fringed coat and her brown velvet riding jacket.

Heat continued to simmer in the air. Sweat plastered her thin blouse to her torso. There wasn't a speck of shade to be had. Kitty used her cuff to mop her brow. "My thick British blood will take some time getting used to American summers."

Wyatt smiled and nudged a can of corn with his pointed boot. "You ain't seen nothing yet." He sobered. "Sorry to get so quiet on you this afternoon."

She sympathized with the need to heal that had caused

him to curl into himself. Selfishly she missed his playful carrying on.

She toed the bag of coffee beans with her knee-high riding boot. "Wouldn't it be lovely to cool our feet in the creek before fixing a bite to eat? Your other choice is to allow me to cook for you."

He gave her a quick hug. "I think I'm starting to love you."

"What?" She squawked like a hen. "What just happened?"

"Nothing," he said, his grin roguish. "If you promise not to cook, I'll do anything you ask."

Her body hummed from the embrace. What would it feel like to be wrapped up for hours in his massive arms? London Bridge, where had that indelicate thought come from? "The stew was rather horrible."

He clutched at his throat and pretended to gag.

She laughed at him and herself. Knowing when to take him seriously was most difficult. There was no reason to get heated. The hug had been a friendly gesture, as was the mention of love. A passing fancy. Nothing more.

He made for the creek. "That water looks mighty refreshing." He plopped down on the flat shelf of rock and tugged off his cowboy boots.

She joined him, anticipating the bliss of dipping her feet in the pool of cold water. The deeper water out in the middle looked especially inviting. "If I were alone, I would be tempted to go for a swim."

Boots and socks tossed carelessly aside, he thumbed his suspenders off his shoulders and worked open the buttons on his shirt as he climbed to his feet. "What's stopping you?" He peeled his shirt off and cast it aside.

The marble statues adoring the gardens of Somerset's landed gentry were quite fascinating, but they paled compared to the sight of real flesh and muscle sculpted over a bank-vault-sized chest. Except that the statues' torsos weren't marred with bullet scars. She swallowed. "I don't know how to swim. And even if I did, it wouldn't be proper."

He reached for the buttons on his fly. "If you haven't noticed—"

Alarmed, she squeezed her eyes closed. "What are you doing?"

His denim pants hit the ground with a slap, followed by the loud splashing of water. "Hoo wee, the water feels right nice."

She cracked open one eye and found him floating on his back in the middle of the creek. He was still clad in white underclothes from the waist down. Thank goodness. She opened the other eye. "Was disrobing really necessary?"

He grinned. "I like them fancy words you use. And I wasn't showing off for you. I just don't want to sleep in wet clothes."

Enamored with his cowboy twang, she couldn't fault his logic. "That is rather sensible, I suppose."

He paddled in a lazy circle. "Do you want me to shut my eyes while you...*disrobe*?"

Telling herself she wasn't scandalized, she sat and tugged off one riding boot. "I do not plan to join you."

"Why not?"

"It would not be proper."

He swam in the opposite direction. "You sound like Red Calder. Back in the day, Jeb and me and some of the other boys would sneak off to swim in the creek. For some reason, Red was dead set against it. But when it got blazing hot, we'd risk getting cussed out."

Unsure if she should be complimented or insulted at his comparing her to a cattle rustler, it gave her the opportunity to ask a burning question. "How did you end up at Hole-in-the-Wall working for a cattle rustling gang?"

He shrugged. Sunlight glittered on the water rippling away from his broad shoulders. "After my first ma and daddy died, I wandered town to town."

His matter-of-fact tone shocked. "How old were you?"

"Four years older than Wally. Plenty big enough to take care of myself."

"Said the man who became a cattle rustler." Her words reflected her horror for his sake, rather than any judgment.

Wyatt flipped onto his stomach and glided toward her. "You might have noticed I'm a bit of an adventure seeker? So, I decided to cross over into Nebraska to have a look see."

"Because playing with fire is such good fun," she mumbled, praying he wouldn't come any closer.

The twinkle in his eyes rivaled the sun. "And I came across Red Calder at the Bucket of Blood Saloon."

"A fine establishment, I'm sure."

His smile was brilliant. "You have a fine sense of humor, Kitty-Girl."

Her skin prickled with heat. Setting her second boot beside the first, she scooted closer to the water. "Whereas yours is strange. Please swim back to the middle of the creek and finish your story, while I soak my feet."

He floated in place. "Aren't you gonna take your stockings off first?"

Aghast at the suggestion—not even Milton had seen her bare feet—she dug a handkerchief from her pocket, wet it, and dabbed her face and neck with the gloriously cool water. "Do not concern yourself with me, Mr. Haven. Pray, go on." She liked calling him by his first name, but distancing herself by reverting to a formal address seemed necessary at the moment.

"Call me Wy. In case you've forgotten, we're married."

Flustered at being so close to his half-naked body, she did not need that reminder. "And so you met Mr. Calder at the Bucket of Blood Saloon."

Merriment danced in his eyes. "Come to find out, I was real good at cattle rustling. Red said he never saw a better handler of Longhorns. I might still be a cattle rustler if Pa Malcolm and Ma Viola hadn't taken me in. Not that I was happy about them shooting me to get my attention."

She blinked. "Who shot you? Red?"

"Nope." He pointed to a scar puckering his shoulder. "Ma's bullet hit here. Pa's went through my calf. They didn't do it on purpose. It was just bad timing. Me and the rest of Red Calder's boys got caught in some crossfire between Blackwell's men and Pa and Ma and some other small nesters."

"Small nesters?" she asked, thrown off by the term.

"That's what modest ranching outfits like Sweet Creek Ranch are called. Anyways, when the dust cleared, I learned Red Calder had hightailed off without me. Pa and Ma took me home and doctored me. After that I became one of their second-chance boys. I was sixteen and cocky and mouthy and a real handful, but Pa and Ma never—"

A green-scaled fish crested the water a short way off.

"Hoo wee, he was a big one," Wyatt said.

Dipping the handkerchief again, she lifted it to her neck and squeezed out the water and sighed at the cool relief. "It's seldom this hot in London or Somerset."

He stood and strode toward the ledge shelf. "Put your feet in. That will cool you off right quick."

The beads of water rolling down his bare skin were mesmerizing. What would it be like to married to a cowboy for real? She moistened her parched lips. "I'm working my way there."

He hoisted himself out of the water and stood over her, white cotton underclothes clinging to muscled thighs. "You look as though you're about to expire from the heat."

She looked away. London Bridge, he was a giant of a man. "Go fix the food and I will be right—"

He scooped her off the ground.

She pushed against his solid chest. His skin was surprisingly smooth. "What are you doing?"

He stepped off the ledge and waded into the creek. "Trust me. You'll thank me for this."

"Put me down," she demanded.

He smiled winningly. "If you say so."

"Not h—" Arms spiraling, she plunged into the

freezing mountain-fed stream. Finding her feet, she surfaced spurting water. She glanced down. Her skin was visible through the thin blouse. She crossed her arms. "You big brute."

Wyatt swam just out of reach looking proud of himself. "Admit it. You're happy I tossed you in."

London Bridge! What woman would want to put up with a lifetime of Wyatt's boyish antics? Not her. A proper British man was her idea of a good husband. Not an uncivilized cowboy.

Chapter Twenty

Two days into her stay at Rosewood Ranch, Kitty was thoroughly convinced the move to Wyoming from Britain would prove the making of her happiness. Henrietta, or Hen, as she was known to friends, walked with her arm looped with hers on a tour of an airy stable lined with stalls still smelling of new wood.

Petite and industrious as a hummingbird, Hen had arranged for a letter to be sent to Milton and Mother informing them of Kitty's whereabouts and inviting them to the ranch if they wished to take part in her search for an appropriate husband.

Henrietta's American husband, Theodore Rochester, had dashed off a letter to Beau Blackwell on her behalf, offering three times the going price to buy back her ponies.

The stable boy riding to Aurora would also have telegrams sent to the pseudo royalty of the American polo pony world, suggesting a visit to Rosewood Ranch to meet Miss Cathryn Cliffton. Her sizable inheritance, coupled with her bloodlines to Britain's landed gentry had garnered immediate interest. Henrietta was lining up visits from potential husbands as efficiently as she would beaus on a dance card. Sons, nephews, and cousins from American dynasties filled the list.

Meanwhile, Kitty engrossed herself with every aspect of the polo pony ranch. She had been enchanted from first sight. The acres of white painted fences. The red-shingled verandas gracing the sprawling log house, bunkhouses, sheds, and out-buildings. The massive fieldstone chimney anchoring the main house. All of it lovely and horsey.

Mother and Milton would hate living here.

Kitty would happily stay for the rest of her life.

The two-story tall doors at the back of the barn overlooked a yellow-green polo field, guarded by a stand of Cottonwoods. The fingers of the bare branches pointed to the jagged peaks of the Bighorn Mountains.

Kitty halted, the beauty of the ranch forgotten, her eyes only for Wyatt and the magnificent Quarter Horse Charger as they raced across the close-mowed polo field. Her breath caught as Wyatt lifted off the saddle and executed a series of dangerous tricks in brilliant fashion.

Wyatt regained his seat, and his indistinct words of praise for Charger drifted to them as they loped away in the direction of the white-capped mountains.

Henrietta shaded her eyes. "That's a couple of fine studs you hitched up with."

"You got that right, ma'am," Kitty replied, copying Hen's outlandish attempt at cowboy-speak.

They hugged and laughed.

Kitty kissed Hen's rosy cheek. "I have missed you so."

"I could not be happier you came." Henrietta looped

arms again. "Nosy ninny that I am, I am dying to ask if Wyatt has tried to steal any kisses?"

"When we were wed." Kitty's toes curled recalling the maple-flavored kiss that had gone on and on. "But it wasn't special or earth-shaking."

A knowing look in her eyes, Henrietta smiled. "I say you ought to drag that cowboy of yours into a dark corner and encourage him to have another attempt at impressing you."

Kitty's face heated. "You are impossible, Henrietta."

"Do it. You know you want to."

Kitty wished she possessed half her friend's spunk. "You were always the one flirting in the corners with the boys."

Henrietta squeezed her arm. "This is the modern world. Marrying a man without knowing if you like his kisses is plain barbaric. You know I am right."

Wyatt's kisses would be as wild and untamed as the man. "I shall be happy to make a practical marriage."

"Dear, this is the new world. You can marry for love."

"I do not love Wyatt."

Henrietta fluttered her eyelashes. "Who said anything about Wyatt?"

Kitty stamped her foot. "You know what I mean."

Henrietta's eyes lost a bit of their brilliance. "Don't sacrifice happiness to a false sense of duty. Consider all the possibilities. That is all I am asking, dear."

False sense of duty. The accusation rang in Kitty's ears. Why was she seeking a husband from among the American elite? Who was she trying to impress? What did she hope to gain? Kitty stared in the direction Wyatt had gone. "You have done it again, Hen. You have left me speechless with your unique view of matters."

Her friend offered a sympathetic smile. "I dare say, both your mother and mine were relieved when I and my modern notions sailed off to America."

Kitty hugged her. It was safe to say neither of their mothers would have considered marrying an American cowboy, much less doing it for love. "Never change, Hen. You are perfect just the way you are."

Hen's tinkling laugh was pure joy. "I ought to be thanking you instead of lecturing. My choices will appear quite conservative and dull compared to you running off with a cattle rustler and would-be trick rider."

Nervous laughter bubbled up. "The scandal of it all."

Not one for standing in one place too long, Henrietta took her hand. "I must have your opinion on the pride and joy of Rosewood. A young foal that my husband and I believe will make as splendid a polo pony as any born this season in Somerset. Though your mind will be abuzz with thoughts of kissing Wyatt, please nod and agree when I praise my handsome pony."

Kitty hurried to keep up as Hen dragged her along. "You are impossible."

"I am," Henrietta said without a hint of remorse.

London Bridge, Hen couldn't have been more correct. The whole time her friend extolled the virtues of the prized foal, her mind was occupied with questions, both exciting and difficult.

Would she be daring and take chances? Such as seeking

the opportunity to kiss Wyatt in a dark corner. Or was she more like her tradition-bound, propriety-loving mother than she cared to admit?

Chapter Twenty-One

The next day, Kitty judged her ponies fit for polo practice. After having enjoyed several days of rest and recuperation, they were raring to go. A sentiment she shared. The sight of them thundering up and down the polo field against the majestic backdrop of the Bighorn Mountains made her heart race.

Kitty, Henrietta, and Theodore took turns knocking the ball with their mallets. That Wyatt was watching her every move on only heightened her elation.

Leaning and twisting in her saddle, Henrietta directed her next shot toward Wyatt.

The ball trundled to a stop at the tips of his cowboy boots.

Hen and Theodore broke away. "Theodore is having Lord Braveheart saddled for Wyatt," Hen called over her shoulder. "You can give your cowboy polo lessons before he expires from boredom."

Kitty drew Lady Winsome to a stop short of the bright white fence. She sensed a growing restlessness in Wyatt. Anytime now, he'd tell her he was going away. She didn't want him to leave. Not yet. "Are you ready to have a go at our British pastime?"

Wyatt leaned against the rails, the fringe on his buckskin jacket and wide-brimmed hat making him look every bit the rugged cowboy. His eyes were as bright as the sun-kissed skies. "Looks easy enough."

She pretended dismay. "You might not say that once you witness the match Theodore has arranged at the end of the week with a neighboring ranch."

All lazy grace, he scooped up the ball and ambled to her. "Kitty-Girl, you don't need me underfoot when the beaus start arriving and buzzing around you like bees to a pretty flower."

Her face heated. "I wish Henrietta had not been quite so enthusiastic on that front. She means well, but tends to act in haste."

His lips curved with a tantalizing smile. "I'd be the last person to criticize on that front." The light faded from his eyes and he pressed the dirt-flecked ball into her hand. "Our fake marriage is a liability now."

Fake marriage. Pained by this necessary conversation, she studied the ball. "Of course. I've abused your generosity and kindness for too long. Henrietta and Theodore said something about a traveling judge who does divorces. And annulments."

"Judge Peck makes an appearance every other month in Aurora. He will know the best means for ending the marriage"

She cringed. "The same judge who married us?"

Wyatt's smile did not light his eyes. "The very same

one. If you don't want to wait till Judge Peck comes north, we can make a trip to Cheyenne."

She bit her lip and eyed the remote mountain range with longing. "I don't want to consider the stir it would cause if we were to return to Cheyenne."

"You won't get any argument from me." Wyatt exhaled heavily. "It's probably best if I head out for Aurora. I can make arrangements for the divorce and congratulate Beau Blackwell for cheating death. Not that he'll believe I mean it."

The stable boy had returned from Aurora last evening with the news that Blackwell was making a slow recovery. The report came as a great relief to her conscience. Much as she wanted her ponies, she did not harbor any ill will toward the man.

She dearly hoped the brush with death had given Blackwell a new outlook instead of further hardening his heart. "I cannot thank you enough for all you have done. Henrietta and Theodore have promised to use their high standing in the polo pony community to shame Blackwell into selling the ponies back to me."

Wyatt's hand covered hers. "Divorced or not, I'll remain in Aurora until matters are settled with Blackwell."

Her throat closed. "You don't have to do that."

He squeezed her fingers. "Yes, I do."

Kitty didn't want him to leave. There had to be a way to convince him to stay just a little longer.

Henrietta and Theodore returned with Lord Braveheart saddled and ready.

Kitty surveyed the English saddle and Wyatt's cowboy

attire. "This might not be such a good idea."

Theodore chuckled. "But it will be fun to watch."

Wyatt mounted Lord Braveheart with ease, and a groom handed him a brand-new mallet.

"Whoa doggie," he said, admiring the long-handled club. "Now, what am I supposed to do with this?" He made a few practice swings, and Theodore and Henrietta applauded his form.

Thirty minutes later Wyatt was knocking the ball around the field with ease, making passes, and sending the ball flying between the goalposts. Kitty had trained enough players to recognize natural talent. Wyatt's performance was even more remarkable given the hindrance of the fringed jacket and the cowboy boots that barely fit the stirrups of the English saddle.

He ought to look ridiculous, but she couldn't take her eyes off him.

Wyatt circled back so their horses stood nose to tail. "Polo is right good fun."

She wished she could freeze the moment. The smell of sweat rising from the horses. The perfect blue skies overhead. The comfort of the reins and polo stick gripped in her hands. She nudged Lady Winsome closer. "Are you ready for some real competition?"

Wyatt brightened. "You betcha."

"Speaking of bets, I have one for you Americans." She looked over her shoulder at Henrietta and Theodore. "Hen and I against Wyatt and Theodore. The first to score wins."

Hen clapped. "What is the prize?"

Kitty locked eyes with Wyatt. "A Sunday picnic. If we

win, the men will make the fixings. If they win, we will cook for them."

Wyatt grinned. "Either way, I will have to stay until Sunday. Is that it?"

Shocked at her own boldness, she nodded. "What's a few more days?"

Theodore rode by rubbing his stomach. "I can taste the fried chicken now, Wyatt. How about you?"

Wyatt chuckled. "If Kitty-Girl here is cooking, I say we let them win."

Kitty smiled and swatted his shoulder. "I promise to stay far away from the stove. And what do you mean…*let us win*? Hen and I will do better than win. We will trounce you."

Good humor danced in his eyes. "We'll have to see about that."

Laughing, she urged Lady Winsome forward, joining Henrietta who was perched on a sleek black mare.

Henrietta's face held an *I told you so* gleam. "*Kitty-Girl*, is it?"

"I don't know why he insists on calling me that." But she always felt braver and prettier when he drawled the nickname.

"I like your cowboy," Hen said. "He is good for you."

Before they were set, one of the stable grooms, acting as the umpire, rolled the ball down the centerline for the official throw-in.

Theodore and Wyatt, showing no remorse at catching them off guard, shared a chuckle as they worked the ball down the field.

Kitty raced to cut off Wyatt, while Henrietta pursued Theodore.

Winnie, champion and competitor that she was, quickly caught Wyatt and Lord Braveheart. But Wyatt checked his pony and got off a perfect offside back-hander.

Theodore tracked down the ball. "Bravo."

"Show off," Kitty called charging by, equally impressed.

Wyatt caught up in a blink. "Move aside, slow pokes." Intercepting a sloppy pass, he managed to connect mallet and ball and careened after it. Either Lord Braveheart was putting on a stellar performance or horse and rider were perfectly matched.

The goalposts loomed ahead. Wyatt approached too fast. Seeing her opportunity, Kitty angled Lady Winsome toward the middle of the field as he took a wild swing with his mallet, completely missing the ball. But Lord Braveheart's back hoof clipped the ball, sending it flying through the goalposts.

Theodore whooped and threw his arms in the air.

"Well done," Henrietta called.

Kitty could only laugh.

Circling back to where they were milling, Wyatt wore a puzzled look. "We scored?"

Theodore grinned. "In the polo world that is called a pony goal." As they all dismounted, he wagged his brows at Kitty and Henrietta. "But a win is a win, right, ladies?"

Kitty tossed a challenging look at Wyatt. "Beginner's luck."

"What?" Wyatt said in mock dismay and boxed her

between Lady Winsome and Lord Braveheart.

"We'll leave you two lovebirds to argue this out," Henrietta said, leading her pony away with Theodore by her side.

Wyatt moved closer. "Lovebirds. I like the sound of that."

An unnerving but pleasant hum filled her. She swung her mallet, purposely missing him.

He captured the stick and pulled her near. His warm breath caressed her ear and spilled down her neck. "I'd say a kiss of congratulations is in order. Wouldn't you?"

She gave him a quick peck on the cheek. The witty reply she'd planned melted away at the taste of his salty skin. Needing to steal one quick kiss to satisfy her gnawing curiosity, she cupped his nape and drew his mouth to hers. The tentative exploration of her lips over his ignited a fire. "Kiss me back," she demanded.

His arms enveloped her, and he crushed his mouth onto hers.

She groaned and ran her fingers along his jaw, her skin prickling at the sensation of the stubble.

All was a white-hot blur. She struggled to speak. "More. I want more." Why couldn't she get enough of him? Of this?

He gasped for breath as he trailed kisses down her neck. "This is a bad idea."

She dragged his mouth back to hers. "I don't care."

His husky laugh reverberated through her.

Lady Winsome whinnied in her ear, and Lord Braveheart answered her.

A dose of horse sense was just what was called for.

Breathing heavily, Wyatt broke off the kiss and rested his forehead against hers. "What just happened, Kitty-Girl?"

Surrounded by her ponies and snug in Wyatt's embrace, she felt safe. "I don't know. But I want it to happen again. And soon."

Wyatt chuckled. "You're my kind of girl."

"We are married, so we would be doing nothing improper."

He pulled back. "That's dangerous talk."

It was gloriously dangerous. "Husbands and wives do more than talk."

His blue eyes darkened. "I might have to steal another—"

A series of deep barks assaulted her ears.

Steadying the horses, she spied a yellow dog loping toward them with his tail wagging, followed by a badge-wearing sheriff, a buckskin-clad Indian with waist-length hair, and Milton, looking every bit the proper Englishman.

"Fluff is real friendly," Wyatt said, his tone preoccupied. "Wish I could say the same for my brothers. Boone and White Wolf aren't ones for smiling, so please don't take their standoffishness personal."

Her heart raced and her thoughts jumbled. She couldn't begin to imagine how her brother had come to make the acquaintance of Wyatt's brothers. Or why they were traveling together.

She reached for Wyatt's hand. "They must be bringing bad news."

A bastion of calm, he enfolded her hand in his. "Appears so."

Chapter Twenty-Two

Henrietta and Theodore's ranch house had no formal parlor, but Kitty preferred gathering around the chunky log table to sitting on couches and wing-back chairs where every nervous gesture would be exposed. But the charm of the pine wainscot, wood beams, and the overhead lamp fashioned from antlers failed to cheer her.

Not with Milton sitting beside her and smirking as he examined the room. The insult was lost on Henrietta and Theodore, who were enthralled by Wyatt's brothers. Kitty had asked the couple to join them, as they were among her few allies here.

Wyatt was seated on her other side facing Boone and White Wolf. If she ran across the pair in a dark alley, she would be scared witless. For good reason. They shared the same impenetrable gaze and stone-cold expression. After a single look from White Wolf, even Milton had ceased the flow of rude remarks aimed at her.

And the deadly pair were making a careful study of her. Boone looked more like a bank robber than the sheriff of Aurora. The grainy newspaper images did not do

American Indians justice. White Wolf's beautiful copper-colored skin and jet-black glossy hair were mesmerizing.

Tempted to gnaw her lip, she crossed her feet and tapped her riding boot against the chair leg as Boone explained the reason for the visit.

Beau Blackwell was indeed on the mend and demanding that Wyatt be arrested and put on trial as a horse thief. "You put me in a real bind, Wy," Boone said without heat. "I don't want to arrest you, but I don't see as I have much choice."

Wyatt shrugged. "A posse would've strung me up, no questions asked. I'm happy to take my chances with a judge and jury."

"Or you could go missing until the trouble blows over," White Wolf said, stringing together his first full sentence. "Spend the season trapping in the mountains and talking my ear off."

Boone's lips ticked upward into something that could almost be called a smile. "Running wouldn't be the worst idea. Might be for the best."

Wyatt shook his head. "I promised Miss Cathryn I'd stay until the matter with her ponies was settled."

Kitty leaned forward and grasped his elbow. She would never forgive herself if Wyatt lost his life when he was only guilty of coming to her assistance. "Listen to your brothers. Run. Leave."

Wyatt's hand covered hers. "Don't be worrying about me. I'm good at talking myself out of trouble."

Why did he have to be so frustratingly calm? "If anyone should be arrested and hanged, I am the one. I am the one at fault." She appealed to Boone and White Wolf for support. "I will swear before a judge Wyatt was only trying to help me. I will take full blame."

Something shifted in Boone's dark eyes. "So you're not playing Wyatt for a fool?"

The muscles flexed in Wyatt's arm. "Don't go insulting Miss Cathryn, or I'll have to punch you in the nose."

Boone held up his hand. "There's no reason to get all fired up. I'm just trying to get to the bottom of matters."

She understood Boone's suspicion. "I should have found another way."

Wyatt shook his head. "Miss Cathryn wanted her ponies back and if Blackwell was a gentleman, he would've accepted her offer to buy them back." His eyes met hers, and he spoke with tender affection. "I knew what I was doing then and the same goes for now. I made a promise and I mean to see it through."

She touched Wyatt's sleeve. "We are in this together." Her father had promised her Lady Winsome and the rest of the ponies would belong to her. But that had not been true. Milton told lies all the time. But she could trust Wyatt to keep his word.

The tension went out of his muscles. "If you say so, ma'am."

"I like a man who doesn't talk back," she replied in the same teasing tone.

Milton crossed his pencil-thin legs. "Kitten, should we give you two some privacy?"

She blushed, hating that Wyatt and his brothers had to witness Milton's meanness.

Wyatt narrowed his eyes at Milton. "Talk nice or don't speak."

Milton's mocking smile never left Kitty's face. "I suppose I should work up the energy to challenge your horse-thieving lover to a duel."

Wyatt plunked his gun on the polished pine table. "Say when and where."

Boone and White Wolf placed their guns on the table.

Milton yawned. "Kitten, I fear I will not be able to defend your honor."

"Wyatt and I married before a judge in Cheyenne." A foresight on Wyatt's part that she was grateful for now.

Milton's lips twitched. "My brother-in-law the cattle rustler. How droll."

Wyatt had eyes only for her. "It was a right nice wedding."

While not the nuptials of her dreams, it was a day she would never forget.

The amusement in White Wolf's eyes was the first emotion he'd showed. "You actually married Beau Blackwell's bride?"

"Figures," Boone grumbled.

Wyatt's jaw firmed. "Miss Cathryn loves her ponies more than life. Would you have said no if she asked for help?"

Boone opened his mouth, then snapped it closed.

White Wolf's gaze flicked to Kitty's. "Is it true? Would you die for your horses?"

Her heart beat louder. Why did this feel like the most vital test of her life? "I would. But I was wrong to put

164

Wyatt in danger."

White Wolf nodded. "You did good, Wyatt," he said, but his eyes remained on her. "If you need our help, just ask."

Milton's fingers drummed the table. "Thank you. You can be sure I will take up your offer."

"Shut up, Cliffton," Boone ordered. He turned to Kitty, his eyes softer. "With a brother as worthless as yours I can see why you'd turn to a stranger for help."

"There is no call to be rude, old chap," Milton said, fumbling in his pocket. He dragged out the pilfered snuffbox.

A familiar dread filled Kitty at the sight of her brother indulging in a pinch of his *medicine*. Who knew what flight of fancy would overtake him? Or perhaps he would be rendered comatose. She had not missed the constant worry over his unpredictable moods. "Milton, please behave."

He chuckled. "Poor Kitten. Are you afraid I—"

White Wolf snatched the ornate snuffbox from Milton, retrieved his gun, and walked out of the room.

Milton hurried after White Wolf. "Here now, give that back."

Henrietta got up from her seat and pushed the door closed. "I see Milton's manners have not improved."

Wyatt squeezed Kitty's hand. "Don't worry. Wolf won't hurt him."

Kitty sighed. Surrounded by the three rugged Haven brothers, Milton's emaciated state stood out. He was killing himself. "I fear Milton will be dead before age thirty-five unless something changes."

Sympathy shone in Wyatt's eyes. "Boone and Wolf and I will try to talk some sense into him."

Hope where her brother was concerned didn't come easily. "How wonderful of you. Thank you."

"Welcome to the family, Miss Cathryn," Boone said, tipping his black cowboy hat.

Wyatt's face grew red. "Miss Cathryn and I didn't marry for real."

Why did the confession tear her heart? Of course, the marriage could never be real. Wyatt was a Wyoming cowboy. She was a British heiress. They both needed to concentrate on setting matters right and returning to their respective lives.

She cleared her throat. "Cathryn sounds so formal. Please call me Kitty."

The housemaid entered the room with a rolling teacart.

Henrietta dismissed the maid and flitted around the cart, pouring steaming tea into pink-rose china cups. The beverage's fragrance filled the room. With Kitty's whole life hanging in the balancing, the ritual of serving tea was comforting.

"Milk or sugar for you, Mr. Haven?" Henrietta asked Boone.

"I take my tea black, ma'am," he drawled.

Wyatt brightened. "Two cubes of sugar for me."

In their cowboy garb, Wyatt and Boone ought to look ridiculous balancing the delicate china cups and saucers in their weather-beaten hands, but they appeared perfectly at ease and not self-conscious.

Boone sipped his tea. "Miss Kitty, I'm not sure if word getting out you and Wyatt are married will help or hurt the court case. But we can spare you the difficulty of traveling to Aurora and testifying in court. Your written testimony should be enough."

The light fled from Wyatt's eyes. "That would be safest."

Kitty meant to see the matter through to the end. "I will be traveling to Aurora with you. I will give my testimony in person at the trial. I insist."

Boone nodded his approval. "Judge Peck is due to arrive at the end of the week."

Wyatt shifted in his chair. "Kitty and I need to see the judge about a divorce."

Talk of divorce made Kitty feel hollow. "Our first priority is clearing Wyatt's name.

Boone nodded and drained his tea in one swallow. "Wyatt will be under house arrest. He can stay with me and Maggie in Aurora or with Ty and Ella at Sweet Creek Ranch."

Wyatt stared at her expectantly. "Come to Sweet Creek with me."

There were countless reasons to decline. "That is a kind offer, but it wouldn't be fair to you or your family."

His arm lightly bumped hers. "You said we were in this together."

He could be very persistent. Was this a battle she wanted to win? Truthfully, no. Besides being more than a little curious about the ranch dedicated to rescuing homeless boys, she was not ready to part with him. "Are you sure your family won't mind?"

He grinned. "They're used to expecting the unexpected from me."

She hoped she did not regret giving in.

Perched on the edge of her chair, Henrietta stirred her tea. "Kitty, forgive my nosiness. Have you considered the possibility that Beau Blackwell will refuse to sell the ponies back to you out of spite? Especially now you have agreed to testify on Wyatt's behalf."

Kitty's stomach knotted. "He will return my ponies."

Henrietta reached across the table and squeezed her hand. "I fear Mr. Blackwell is a blackguard."

Wyatt's eyes turned stormy. "If Blackwell refuses to be reasonable, I'll cut a deal. I'll agree to plead guilty and go to prison for a few years in exchange for the ponies."

The thought horrified Kitty. "Prison? No. I will not allow it."

Boone arched a brow. "Wy, that's a drastic offer. These are horses we're talking about."

Henrietta's teacup was poised at her lips. "Those ponies are Kitty's happiness. They are her whole life."

Wyatt nodded. "The point of the last week was to rescue Kitty's ponies. A job that ain't done yet."

Shame reverberated through Kitty. Did Wyatt and Henrietta believe her that selfish? Could she blame them? Her recent actions had certainly been self-centered. She accused Milton of leaving rack and ruin in his wake as he crashed through life. Was she more like Milton than she wanted to admit?

Wyatt pressed closer. "No one will blame you for doing

what's best for your ponies."

She wouldn't allow him to hang or go to prison. "No. You cannot make such a deal."

"I like it when you're feisty, Kitty-Girl." Warm affection filled his voice. "We'll find a way to beat Blackwell. You'll have your ponies. And I'll escape the hangman's noose. What do you say?"

Was this what love felt like? Fear, elation, risk, comfort and too many other emotions to count. Did she want a future with Wyatt? Was he ready to take on the responsibility of helping her establish and operate a champion polo pony ranch? One thing was certain. Time was running out for them. "Give me an hour to see to my ponies and packing. Then I will be ready to ride to Aurora, and on to Sweet Creek Ranch."

Chapter Twenty-Three

The weather deteriorated on the four-hour journey from Rosewood Ranch to Aurora. With the daylight quickly fading, Wyatt turned up his collar against the spitting sleet as he, Kitty, Boone, White Wolf, and Milton Cliffton exited the stables.

"I thought it was spring," Cliffton complained.

Wyatt shrugged. "That's Wyoming for you." Spring came to the mountains in fits and starts, with the tease of warm sunny days retreating to cold dampness.

The windows of Bailey's Emporium and the Last Chance Trading Post were dark, but lights and noise spilled from the saloons. Cowpokes eager to work the spring roundup were arriving daily, turning the normally sleepy town into a lively hive.

Wyatt swallowed against the lump in his throat. He thought he'd said his last goodbye to Aurora and Sweet Creek Ranch. He was back. But for how long?

White Wolf's hand settled briefly on his shoulder. "Until next time." He disappeared into the shadows. No telling when White Wolf make his next appearance. It could be days, weeks, or months before the family saw him again.

The parting gesture was a comfort.

"White Wolf seems like a shifty fellow," Cliffton remarked. "But at least he returned my snuffbox."

Wyatt flexed his balled hands and led the way toward Johnson's Boardinghouse.

As they passed the Rawhide Saloon, Cliffton broke away. "Don't wait up for me, Kitten."

"Milton," Kitty called after him.

Not heeding his sister, he disappeared through the batwing doors.

Wyatt followed and narrowly avoided bowling over Beau Blackwell and his ranch foreman Amos Little at the foot of the stairway.

"Wyatt Haven," Blackwell bellowed. "You'll be the death of me yet."

Amos Little drew his revolver. "If it ain't the horse thief."

The tinny piano music died and the seventy-five plus saloon patrons stared in silence.

Wyatt freed his gun. Blackwell was supposed to be holed up at his ranch, resting his heart. What could have brought him to town? "Don't do nothing stupid, Amos."

Amos's chuckle wasn't friendly. "You're the stupid one for stealing them horses."

Boone and Kitty entered the saloon. Boone held her arm before she could rush forward.

Cliffton hovered near the faro table.

Wyatt's pulse galloped. Hoo wee, he was back in

Aurora for less than twenty minutes and trouble had already found him.

Fear shadowed Kitty's face. "Wyatt, please be careful."

Blackwell looked thinner and paler, and his droopy mustache dominated his face. "Some proper Englishwoman you are, consorting with a cattle rustler and outlaws of every stripe to steal my property."

Kitty's chin rose. "If I aspired to be a proper Englishwoman, you Mr. Blackwell, would be the last man I would choose to marry." Her British accent sliced like sword. "Wyatt Haven is more of a gentleman than you or Milton will ever be."

"Is that so?" Blackwell wore a scoffing look. "Perhaps I should start addressing you as Horse Thief Kitty?"

"I've always preferred Kitten," Cliffton observed drolly.

Wyatt drew back his shoulders. "Be careful how you speak to my wife."

Blackwell's face pinched. "You're welcome to keep the tart. I don't want someone else's leftovers."

Kitty tugged free of Boone's hold and stormed toward Blackwell. "Tart? How dare you call me that?"

Wyatt caught her around the waist. "Whoa up."

Kitty settled against him, but continued to mutter over the insult.

Cliffton grinned. "Wyatt, tell me if you are going to throw Kitty over your shoulder and carry her out of the Rawhide. I want to know if I should find a photographer to capture the picture."

"If I'm going to hogtie anyone, it will be you," Wyatt

growled.

Cliffton fetched the fancy gold snuffbox from his jacket breast pocket. "It is unfortunate I will not have Tammy coming to my rescue. Now there is a delightful woman." He turned to Blackwell. "Mr. Blackwell, if your poor health makes it impossible for you to *entertain* Tammy, I should be happy to take her off your hands."

The saloon patrons had a good laugh.

Blackwell scowled with new ferocity. "Amos, if Cliffton utters one more word shoot him."

Amos freed his second revolver and aimed it at Cliffton. "Sure thing, boss."

"Milton, do remember this is the Wild West," Kitty pleaded.

"I figured you might still be angry over that picture in the *Daily News*," Wyatt said, in a bid to distract Blackwell. "What can I do to make amends? Sending flowers don't fit the bill. I could walk down Cheyenne's main avenue wearing a dunce cap. Or I could write a note of apology."

More laughter rolled through the saloon.

Blackwell's face turned barn-red. "We'll see how funny you find it if I horse whip you."

Amos turned both his revolvers on Wyatt. "Or I could fill you full of holes."

Wyatt pushed Kitty behind his back. There he went running his big mouth, endangering those he loved.

Boone stepped into the middle of the fray, lamplight dancing over his Colt .45 Peacemaker and sheriff's badge. "Put the guns away."

Amos's face screwed up in defiance.

"Do as he says," Blackwell ordered.

Amos obeyed, but continued to glower at Wyatt. "I'd stay out of dark alleys if I was you."

Wyatt holstered his revolver, and met Blackwell's hard stare. "I'm glad you been making a good recovery. I'm serious about making peace."

Kitty barged forward. "Save yourself the drudgery of a trial. Sell the ponies to me and we can put this unfortunate affair to rest."

Blackwell's unbending posture spoke volumes. "Darling, that's not the deal we made."

Wyatt ground his molars. "You best use Miss Cathryn or Mrs. Haven, unless you're wanting a lesson in manners."

Kitty patted Wyatt's arm without taking her eyes off Blackwell. "What do you want?"

"I'll drop all the charges against Wyatt and sell the ponies to you. But—" The insufferable man pulled a red checkered handkerchief from his back pocket and blew his nose loudly.

Kitty bounced on her toes. "But what?"

Blackwell's smile would look at home on the devil. "I keep Lady Winsome."

The color drained from Kitty's face. "Not Winnie."

Blackwell stuffed the handkerchief in his back pocket. "It's your choice." He cast a triumphant look at Wyatt. "If you ask me, you should keep horse rather than save Wyatt's sorry hide."

A low buzz of speculation filled the air.

Kitty leaned heavily against Wyatt. "I cannot choose.

Do not…" Her breath was labored. "Do not make…me…choose."

Rubbing her back, Wyatt didn't have to think twice about his answer. "We'll see you in court."

Blackwell couldn't have looked more smug. "Milton Cliffton's sworn testimony will bury you."

Wyatt glanced at Kitty's brother for confirmation, wondering at the size of the bribe Blackwell had offered the worthless man.

"Don't blame me," Cliffton said, fumbling his snuffbox open and securing a pinch of the toxic tobacco mix. "You are the one who corrupted my sister and turned her into a horse thief."

Kitty gaped at her brother. "Milton, you cannot testify. Wyatt could hang."

He inhaled a nostril full of snuff, and his eyelids fluttered in bliss. "Give Mr. Blackwell your pony."

Kitty's distress deepened. "What do you hope to gain?"

He polished the blue-enamel box with his lapel and examined the results. "I want you to marry a rich American who has numerous grand homes suitable for entertaining your indolent brother for interminably long visits."

Wyatt might not understand all the man's highfalutin words, but he understood rudeness when he heard it. He pointed a warning finger. "Treat your sister with respect. Do you understand me?"

But Cliffton was staring at the top of the stairway. His mouth crinkled with a wicked smile. "What have we here?"

All eyes went to the infamous lady cardsharp, the Jewel of Texas, gracefully descending the stairs, decked out in a yellow gown, her blond hair as splendid as spun gold.

Wyatt hadn't forgotten about the lucky gold coin Cliffton had stolen from her, and the Jewel wouldn't forget either. Thunderation! The last thing he needed was more trouble.

Beau Blackwell offered Jewel his arm when she reached the bottom step. "My dear," he said, oozing oily charm. "Do you want to make the announcement, or shall I?"

Jewel's smile didn't reach her eyes. "Please do."

Blackwell grasped her waist, marking her as his woman. "The Jewel of Texas and I are the new owners of this fine establishment."

Wyatt could only blink. Blackwell and the Jewel in business together. The day was chock full of surprises.

Jewel slipped around Blackwell and swept toward the bar. "Slim, drinks all around on me."

The announcement was greeted with cheers and whistles.

Wyatt took advantage of the ensuing celebration to whisk Kitty out of the saloon.

She stared over her shoulder. "I do hope Milton stays out of trouble."

A cold wind buffeted Wyatt's buckskin jacket. "If Milton is wise, he'll leave town."

Kitty sheltered against him. "Heaven help us all if our welfare depends on Milton's wisdom."

Boone caught up with them as they stepped off the

porch. "Hold up."

Wyatt tensed. "We've had enough jolting news for one night."

Boone gave a curt nod. "Get ready for some more. The telegraph operator pulled me aside just now. Judge Peck is due to arrive in Aurora on Friday."

"Four days," Kitty said, her distress evident in her furrowed brow.

Wyatt turned up his collar against the icy breeze striking his neck. *Four days.* Shoot, that was a wink in time. The high stakes were dizzying. Kitty's ponies, the trial, the end of the fake marriage. Would there even be time for a visit to Sweet Creek Ranch?

Why this vital need to take Kitty home to meet his family? What did he hope to accomplish? Why was he certain this was the remedy to the plague of troubles hounding them?

Chapter Twenty-Four

During the short walk to Johnson's Boardinghouse, Wyatt warned Kitty that the Jewel of Texas might cause trouble for Milton on account of his stealing her lucky gold coin. Kitty shared the details the theft of the snuffbox and the disgrace that had chased them from London.

Wyatt reached for her hand upon reaching the glum shadows of the boardinghouse's lamp-lit doorway, where her mother and brother had found rooms for their short stay in Aurora. He hated the thought of parting for the night. Did she feel the same? He didn't like the heavy silence between them. From her gloom you'd think someone had died. "Your brother is a rotten apple. Are you sure you're related?"

She managed a weak smile. "Very well put. My mother doesn't help. She encourages his worst impulses." Her face crumpled. "How unsporting of me to criticize my brother and mother when I am equally selfish and uncaring."

Desperate to comfort her, he started to gather her into his arms. "Don't say that. Your brother is a thief and a scoundrel. You are good, and all that's lovely."

She put a restraining hand on his chest. Tears pooled in her dark eyes. "How can you say that when I put my ponies' welfare above your life? I am far more selfish than Milton at his worst."

Her pain cut a swath through his heart. "Don't talk like that. Blackwell was hateful and cruel to ask you to choose between keeping Lady Winsome and dropping the horse-thieving charges against me."

She hid her face in her hands. "I am ashamed of myself for not immediately doing what was right." She lifted her head, looking as wild eyed as a horse trapped in a canyon. "Take me back to the saloon. I will tell Mr. Blackwell that I will accept the deal. Winnie will forgive me. I pray she will forgive me."

Wyatt's muscles quivered at the restraint required to remain motionless. "Kitty-Girl, you're killing me. I want to hold you. Come to me. Allow me to comfort you."

Bursting into tears, she launched herself into his arms. "I am sorry. So sorry."

He held her tight, pressing kisses to her forehead. "It'll be okay." He repeated the words over and over, needing to believe it.

Her tears finally slowed. "What if it isn't? What if the jury decides against you?"

He tilted her chin up and kissed her tenderly. "Blackwell won't win. We won't allow it. I'm going to go free and we will save your ponies. All of them."

Hope and fear warred in her eyes. "I want to believe you."

He would deliver on the promise. He had to. "I'm a Haven. And Havens always—

The door opened abruptly, and a shrill voice pierced his ears. "Cathryn, what is the meaning of this?"

He and Kitty broke apart.

She dried her eyes on a flowered hankie. "Wyatt, my mother, Mrs. Elaine Cliffton. Mother, allow me to introduce you to my husband, Wyatt Haven."

Wyatt's ear perked. *Husband.* Wasn't that interesting. She could have introduced him as a cattle rustler, or ranch man, or would-be Wild West trick rider.

Mrs. Cliffton stared down her nose at Wyatt as though inspecting an insect or some other disagreeable pest. Wearing a fancy navy-blue dress and draped in emerald and gold jewelry, she could have stepped out of the society page. "I suggest we finish this conversation in the sitting room."

A few moments later they stood in a tiny room dominated by frayed plaid upholstered furniture and ugly flowered wallpaper. Wyatt wasn't sure about the proper way of greeting a grand lady, but figured it couldn't hurt to remove his Stetson. "Pleased to meet you, ma'am."

Mrs. Cliffton's eyes flicked to Kitty. "Husband? Why was I not consulted? What are his family ties? Please tell me he comes from a banking or real estate dynasty. I would even take a man coming from new money."

Kitty groaned. "Mother."

He preferred brutal honesty. "I'm sorry to disappoint, but my folks were poor pioneers. Whereas, my experience runs to cattle ranching and the occasional rustling of

Longhorns. And polo ponies. Ain't that right?" he asked Kitty with a playful wink.

Kitty's brow smoothed. "Wyatt is taking me to his mountain ranch to meet his family. I don't know how much money or land he and his family have. And I don't care."

Wyatt felt like a million bucks. Kitty wasn't talking like she meant to divorce. Of course, he'd gain a mother-in-law who would need to be charmed. "Mrs. Cliffton, you are welcome to come with us. The ranch is a bit rustic, but us Havens will go out of our way to ensure you are comfortable."

Twitching and staring like a perplexed rabbit, Mrs. Cliffton snapped open an ugly yellow fan and batted the air. "What have you done with Milton?"

"Nothing," Wyatt replied cautiously.

She turned to Kitty. "Where is your brother? He is supposed to be with you."

Kitty sighed. "He stopped at one of the saloons to gamble."

Mrs. Cliffton's eyes filled with alarm. "And you left him behind?"

Wyatt was indignant on Kitty's behalf. "Milton deserted your daughter."

Mrs. Cliffton didn't bother to look at him. "Cathryn, you must go back for Milton. Or he might disappear for days."

"It will not be the first time," Kitty said, her tone resigned. "I wish you would accept Wyatt's invitation."

Mrs. Cliffton drew back in horror. "Milton needs me.

What if he falls ill again? Who will give him his medicine? Feed him? Bathe him?"

Kitty glanced at Wyatt briefly, embarrassment writ on her reddening face. "Milton is a grown man. He should be taking care of you."

Mrs. Cliffton fanned her face more briskly. "Go ahead. Be selfish. Traipse off to the mountains with strangers rather than stay to help me and your brother."

Wyatt had heard enough. "Your son is a—"

Kitty tugged him by the elbow. "Wyatt, I will walk you to the door."

He allowed her to tow him out of the room.

Mrs. Cliffton called after them, "Cathryn, do ask Mr. Haven to search for Milton."

Kitty made no reply to the request. Reaching the front door, her shoulders fell. I am sorry you had to see that."

Milton Cliffton's and Mrs. Cliffton's lack of concern for Kitty was appalling. "I see why you spend so much time with your horses."

She kneaded the spray of flowers embroidered on the corner of the hankie. "Before my father died it was easier. Father doted on me and mother spoiled Milton. It worked and felt fair. I adored my father. And I thought he felt the same. But…" her voice trailed off.

Wyatt wanted to learn all there was to know about her. "Tell me."

Pain flared in her eyes. "Father spent his last hours bemoaning the fact, his heir, Milton, would waste and destroy his life's work. I promised to do all in my power to prevent that. But we both knew the situation was hopeless. And with his last breath, my father looked at me in disappoint and said, *'Why could you not have been a boy?'"*

Wyatt rubbed her arms and kissed her forehead. "I'm sorry." The words seemed inadequate, but he didn't know what else to say.

He felt a shiver go through her. She said, "I hated that I had in any way been a disappointment to him. At first, I told myself he didn't mean what he said. But watching the estate waste away these last eight years under Milton's care, I see the truth of Father's words."

Wyatt held her hands. "But your ponies have never failed or betrayed you."

Tears shone in her eyes. "Thank you for understanding. And for helping me save my ponies."

Her mother, father, and brother had failed her. But he wouldn't. He wanted Kitty to know the joy and comfort of a caring and loving family. He wanted to be her family. He wanted to hear her introduce him as *my husband* for the rest of their days.

He ached to hold her in his arms the whole night long. He hated the thought of leaving her behind. The best he could offer for the moment was to cheer her up. "Lady Winsome is going to love Sweet Creek Ranch. Once she's pranced in the green pastures and eats the sweet grass, she might never want to leave."

Kitty sighed. "That sounds lovely."

Did she feel the same about her home as he did? "Will you miss England?"

He listened in fascination as she described the large

estate in Somerset. She had less to say about London, only that she was separated from her ponies.

She squeezed his hand. "America is my home now."

She wouldn't miss her old life. The thought eased his mind. "I'm right happy about that, Kitty-Girl."

"So am I."

"I hope you don't mind my saying you are as pretty as a filly."

A hint of pink tinged her ivory cheeks. "Will there be time before Judge Peck arrives to visit the ranch?"

A week ago, Wyatt didn't know if he'd ever see the ranch and his family again. Now he couldn't wait to return home and introduce Kitty to the people and place he loved most in this world.

With the rugged beauty of the Bighorn Mountains as a backdrop, he was scheming his last rustling adventure. Only instead of rustling cattle, he intended to corral a bride. How difficult could it be to woo a woman? Mountain picnics, day-long trail rides, evenings kissing on the porch swing, and dozens of bouquets of spring flowers ought to do the trick.

That he had less than four days to pull off the feat put a hitch in his giddy-up.

"It's a one-hundred-mile round trip," he confessed. After the hectic travels she'd endured over the last several weeks, he'd understand if she preferred to stay put to rest and recover. Tempted to beg, he instead went with a hopeful look. "If we leave early tomorrow morning, we could spend a day, or two, at the ranch."

"What time should I be ready?" she answered without

hesitation.

He grinned. "Yeehaw. You *are* my kind of girl."

After they settled on a time, she gave him a good-night kiss on the cheek.

But Wyatt's night was far from over. He set himself on a mission to track down Cliffton and talk some sense into the pompous fool.

Chapter Twenty-Five

Wyatt spent the bulk of the journey to Sweet Creek Ranch assaulted by Cliffton's rambling complaints. Needless to say, the conversation with him the evening before had not gone according to plan.

Finding him well on his way to losing a small fortune at the faro table, Wyatt had dragged the drug-addled man into the alley behind the Wagon Wheel. Cliffton, who was determined to return to the *hot* cards, didn't hear a word of Wyatt's lecture.

But he got Cliffton's attention by wrapping him up mummy-like with a rope and confiscating the fancy snuffbox and the Jewel's lucky gold coin. Cliffton had gone berserk, making all sorts of outlandish threats, plus, a few that were unnervingly dead serious.

Wyatt had decided the only answer was to sober up the man. Kitty deserved to have at least one conversation with her brother minus the influence of the coca-laced snuff. The same went for Cliffton testifying at the trial. Wyatt wouldn't hang based on the testimony of a delusional addict.

Cliffton had squawked like a hen all the way to Doc Craig's place. Doc had said it could take as long as two weeks for Cliffton to return to a *normal* state. They didn't have that many days to spare, so the four they had would have to do. Doc assured him the trip to Sweet Creek Ranch wouldn't do Cliffton any physical harm. It was Doc's opinion keeping Cliffton as far away from civilization as possible would be best. Remote they could do.

Cliffton had spent the hour since their arrival at Sweet Creek brooding in a corner of the main room, far from the tree-length pine table swarming with a noisy gaggle of children and adults.

Kitty, having failed to coax her brother to join them, kept a wide-eyed gaze on the goings-on of a Haven family meal. Was she just curious, or anxious?

A fine Englishwoman, she stood out like a diamond-crusted tiara amid the rustic post and beam ceiling, fieldstone fireplace, and a kitchen dominated by a squat black stove. Drawn to the shiny and sparkling, Wyatt found the result just dandy.

Though quiet, Kitty didn't reek of Milton's snobbery or conceit. Wyatt thought her natural reserve her most appealing trait. In consequence, he received double the pleasure in her smiles and laughter in response to his latest antics.

Tonight, he had competition for her attention. Pride for his family and home thundered in his heart. Ty and Ella, constituting the heart and soul of the Haven family in the wake of Pa Malcolm and Ma Viola's untimely deaths, couldn't have been more welcoming.

A ranch man from the tips of his scuffed cowboy boots to his silver bolo tie, Ty engaged Kitty in a conversation centered on the differences between running a cattle ranch and a polo pony operation.

Ella, a mix of southern belle and tiny tornado, fussed over her three-year old son and year-old twin daughters, while supervising Wally's first cooking lesson. And all the while she made sure Kitty enjoyed a generous dollop of down-home hospitality.

The front door flew open, and the youngest second-chance boys raced to the washstand to clean away the dirt from the evening chores.

"Sweet biscuits and jam," Ella exclaimed, as Billy, Juan, and Tucker peppered Wally with sincere questions and pretend insults about the results of the beef stew bubbling on the stove. Ma Viola had insisted the first generation of second-chance boys—Wyatt, Ty, Boone, White Wolf, Levi, and Ace—knew how to cook and sew as well as read and write.

"Miss Cathryn will think we're raising heathens," Ella said, eyes shining with love and pride.

Billy, Juan, and Tucker hurried to their seats at one end of the pine table.

Wyatt unlimbered legs stiff from a long day of riding and joined Wally at the stove. He leaned over the pot and sniffed. "Smells edible."

The boy hooked his thumbs in his suspenders. "Cutting the potatoes and carrots was the trickiest part."

Wyatt dipped a ladle in the gravy and took a cautious taste.

Wally and the rest of the family watched, clearly anxious for his verdict.

"Mm...mm," Wyatt said, rubbing his belly. "I might have to go back for seconds tonight." The stew could use more salt and pepper and a few lumps floated atop the gravy, but Wyatt knew Wally would remember this as the tastiest meal he'd ever eaten.

Using two dishcloths, Wyatt lifted the large pot. "Take your seat and I'll..." The words died in his throat as he turned and found Seth glaring at him from the other side of the room.

The shadow of Calvin's ghost stood between them as Wally plopped down on the long bench, sitting in Calvin's spot. Wally pushed aside the glass jelly-jar holding Calvin's collection of marbles. Four months had passed since the accident, and time marched ruthlessly on. Wally and future second-chance boys would have no knowledge or memory of Calvin except as the name on a marker in the family cemetery. The jar of marbles stood as a testament, a promise that the rest of the family wouldn't forget.

Seth's eyes cut to Ty. "We have a major fence problem at the upper end of the north pasture. The whole herd looks to have escaped."

Ty hopped to his feet, kissed Ella on the cheek, and headed for the door. "Wyatt, get these boys fed. Then get everyone up to the north pasture."

The door slammed shut behind Ty and Seth, and Wyatt plunked the pot on the table and touched Kitty's shoulder. There went the plans for the picnic and wooing Kitty. "I hate to abandon you, but—"

"I'd like to go with you," Kitty said, her tone closer to a demand than a request.

Cliffton bounded out of his chair. His hair and clothes were a disheveled mess. "Don't go, Kitten. For all we know this caveman plans to knock you over the head and drag you off to Canada."

Wyatt stared in stunned disbelief. "Canada? Caveman?"

Kitty blushed with embarrassment. "Milton, apologize."

"Holy Moly." Wally giggled hysterically along with the other children. Ty and Ella's small son squealed a laugh. "Wyatt does sort of look like a caveman."

Cliffton gave them a scathing look. "Wyatt has been scheming all along to steal my sister and her fortune. In Canada he will be beyond the reach of American law and justice."

The talk of Canada came out of the blue. Wyatt was beyond baffled. He leaned down and spoke into Kitty's ear. "Doc Craig said Milton might talk crazy."

Kitty's shoulders were tight. "The medicine affects him like this. Nothing you say will change his mind."

Ella, her arms wrapped protectively around her twin girls, caught Wyatt's attention. "Take Mr. Cliffton with you to the north pasture. He can see for himself there's no need to worry."

Cliffton frisked his breast pocket and dragged out a steel can of plain mint snuff Doc Craig had recommended to ease the withdrawal symptoms. His murderous frown reflected his feelings over Wyatt confiscating the other snuffbox. But it was the loss of the coca-laced contents energizing his foul mood. "The last thing I need is this oaf and his rooting-tooting cowboy brothers watching over me like a baby."

Wally crossed his eyes in comical fashion, then twirled his finger next to his head to indicate Cliffton was crazy.

The other boys cracked up.

Cliffton's mask of disdain reasserted itself. "What boorish cretins you are."

"Wally," Wyatt chided, picking up the soup ladle. "You and I will be having a talk on manners later."

Wyatt served up a bowl of steaming beef stew for Kitty. Cliffton could kick all he wanted, but he would be coming along for the fence-mending party. "Time to eat up."

The steel snuffbox sailed through the air and cracked against Calvin's jelly jar, splintering the glass. A rainbow of red, blue, green, and yellow marbles cascaded across the pine table. Wyatt jumped to save them. Shards impaled both hands to the sound of marbles pinging off the wood floor.

After that all became a blur—Wally and the other boys scrambling after the marbles, Ella taking charge of the cleanup, Cliffton slinking off.

Kitty held his bloody hands. Her mouth moved, but he couldn't hear the words. His eyes were riveted on the red smeared marbles cradled in his hands. Memories of holding Calvin's broken body flooded in.

A sick foreboding strangled his gut. His foolishness was responsible for one death. He could barely keep himself out of harm's way. What made him think he could keep Kitty safe? Sooner or later he would mess up. He always did.

Chapter Twenty-Six

In the damp gray dawn, a thick blanket of clouds obscured the grandiose view of the Bighorn Mountains. After hours repairing the barbed wire fence, Wyatt stowed the rusty pliers in his back pocket and flexed his bandaged hand.

Two fence posts away, Kitty struggled with the final twist of steel wires on the splice she'd been laboring over for the last quarter hour.

Dead grass crunched underfoot as he made his way to her. Stray wisps of hair danced over her intent features.

She didn't resist when he freed the heavy tool from her hand and finished pinching off the wire. Streaks of dirt stained her brow. A dew of perspiration added brilliance to her apple-red cheeks. She had never looked more beautiful.

"I still find it difficult to believe the destruction of the fence was done on purpose," she said.

They'd arrived in the north pasture the evening before and learned a mile of fencing had been deliberately destroyed. If Seth, Levi, and Ace hadn't caught and chased off Blackwell's men, the amount of damage could have been disastrous.

The "fence war" was being waged across the region between small nesters like Ty, who were fencing in their land and raising domesticated stock such as Herefords, and cattle barons like Blackwell determined to continue herding Texas Longhorns over the open range.

Wyatt suspected his recent actions had gone a long way toward provoking Blackwell to attack Sweet Creek Ranch in this manner. Angry at himself and Blackwell, he ground his teeth and nodded in the direction of the small campsite. "A hearty breakfast and a gallon of cowboy coffee will set us up good."

Not knowing what to expect when he'd left the ranch house the night before, Wyatt had the boys pack bedrolls for everyone and loaded a packhorse with plenty of supplies. Ella arrived early this morning with her three toddlers and set about cooking enough food to feed everyone in Wyoming. Garrett and Ox had just arrived to lend a hand. Miss Ella was making sure they filled their stomachs before heading out to round up Ty's Herefords.

Neighbors also showed up to lend a hand. Wyatt waved to Buck and Ugly Sally as they rode for the west end of the fence. At this rate the fence ought to be mended by nightfall.

Kitty dabbed her neck with her flower-trimmed hankie. "Your American community spirit is admirable."

He chuckled and offered her his elbow. "Blackwell would say us small nesters sticking together is annoying."

Seth glared at him as they approached the campfire. "What happened to your big plans to join a Wild West show?"

Ella, Garrett, and Ox shifted in place, clearly uncomfortable at the hate simmering off Seth.

Kitty squeezed Wyatt's arm. "Will you allow me to change your bandages? My mind will rest easier if I know the cuts are not festering."

One shard had buried deep in his left hand, but the rest of the wounds were superficial. The memory crowding in of the blood-soaked marbles was a heart-wrenching reminder that Seth had every right to detest the sight of him.

He allowed Kitty to lead him to the makeshift log seats where Levi and Ace were yakking it up with Billy, Juan, Tucker, and Wally as their eager audience. Cliffton sat off to one side, his head in his hands as he nursed a headache.

Seth continued to glower at him. He welcomed the distraction of introducing Kitty to Levi and Ace.

Wyatt tugged off his gloves. The cuts still stung, but no fresh blood stained the white gauze bandages. He picked at the edge of one wrap.

Kitty pushed his hand aside and gently unwound the bandage.

Ace leaned forward, inspecting the collection of angry red slices. "It's good you're not squeamish about doctoring wounds, Miss Kitty. 'Cause Wyatt will keep you busy. Wy, did you tell Miss Kitty about the time you jumped off the porch roof and broke your fall on Ma Viola's butter churn?" Ace winked. "That old churn never was same after Pa Malcolm cobbled it back together."

A suppressed smile twitched the corners of Kitty's

mouth. "How dreadful."

Ace grinned. "Wyatt thought so when he had to wash dishes for a month."

Wyatt winced, remembering the well-deserved lecture. "Ma did love that churn."

Levi sat forward on the log. The diagonal scar on his chin exaggerated his frown. "Don't pay no mind to Ace. He's in a feisty mood after learning the Jewel of Texas is in Aurora. As soon as the fence is mended he'll be racing off to lose his money gambling at her table."

Ace crossed his arms in indignant fashion. "I'm not feisty. I was just filling Miss Cathryn in on Wyatt's penchant for messing up."

"You're one to speak," Levi chided. "It's amazing I'm not dead with all the fool tricks you pull."

Ace never was one to walk away from a losing fight. "I wasn't the one who put a rattlesnake in your bed."

Levi squirmed and paled. "Did you have to remind me of the snake?"

Kitty gasped. "Wyatt, you didn't?"

Wyatt shrugged and studied the toes of his boots. "I didn't realize Levi was petrified of snakes."

Levi frowned. "I was surprised. Not petrified. There's a difference."

Ace reached behind Levi and pinched his rear.

Levi jumped and hollered and danced a jig.

Ace tipped his Stetson at Kitty. "Nice to meet you before my brother kills me." Then he sprinted away with Levi in hot pursuit.

Billy, Juan, Tucker, and Wally were laughing so hard,

they were practically rolling on the ground.

Kitty finished wrapping a new bandage on Wyatt's hand. Her warm laugh filled his ears. "You were a rascal as a boy."

Wyatt exhaled heavily. "I wish I could say I've changed."

Ox pushed a mug of coffee into his hand and joined them. "Quit having all this fun without me."

Garrett strolled over wearing a wide smile. "There's never a dull moment when Wyatt is involved."

Wally climbed on a log, his arms flailing to maintain balance. "Ladies and gentlemen, step right up for Mr. Wyatt's Folly Show." His voice rang like a circus announcer.

Sure Seth was hating all the attention he was getting, Wyatt stared into the fire.

A gunshot exploded. The bullet tore the tin coffee mug from Wyatt's hand.

Pandemonium erupted, with everyone exclaiming and talking over each other.

Levi and Ace raced back to the log circle. Ty, Buck, and Ugly Sally charged across the field on their horses.

Wyatt didn't recall standing and embracing Kitty. He examined her and everyone else for harm. "Is anyone hurt?" he asked, his chest tight with fear.

Cliffton's face was white as fresh-fallen snow. "The bullet whizzed by my nose."

Wreathed in smoke, Seth wore a smirk as Miss Ella scolded him and pried the revolver from his hand.

Wyatt charged toward him. "Are you stark raving mad?

You could have killed someone."

Seth's shoulders squared. "The bullet missed Mr. Sissy by a foot."

Wally belly-laughed. "Mr. Sissy. That's a good one."

Cliffton sneered. "Compared to you barbarian cowboys every gentleman in Britain qualifies as a sissy."

Wyatt was two paces from Seth when Ty stepped between them. Garrett and Ox grabbed Wyatt's elbows from behind and held on.

Ty's stern eyes fastened on Wyatt. "What did you do this time?"

The rebuke and the automatic assumption he was at fault gutted Wyatt.

"Wyatt was minding his own business," Ace growled. "Seth is the one looking to get punched in the nose."

Levi nodded in agreement. "Wy was just joking and joshing like he always does."

Wally strutted forward. "Seth doesn't know how to have fun."

"Stop!" Wyatt said.

Seth had made it abundantly clear there wasn't enough room for them both at Sweet Creek Ranch. Wyatt had returned. And his presence was responsible for setting Seth at odds with the family.

What if Kitty or one of the second-chance boys had gotten in the way of the bullet? The image of Calvin flying off the horse flashed through his mind. His foolishness could have gotten another of his loved ones killed. That was something he couldn't live through again.

Chapter Twenty-Seven

Stuffing her belongings into the simple cloth sack that went inside the saddle bag, Kitty reluctantly left behind the cozy ranch-house bedroom. Nothing would make her happier than to spend several more days or weeks in the homey environs of Sweet Creek Ranch, enjoying the company of the Haven family.

But her disappointment was a minor matter.

In the aftermath of the prank gunshot, Wyatt's dependable smiles and playful banter had vanished. Taking all the blame, he made up his mind to depart immediately for Aurora despite his brothers' adamant insistence that Seth was the guilty party.

His withdrawn silence on the return ride to the ranch had filled her with foreboding.

She found him now slumped on the rustic-pine chair facing the wall-size fireplace. Milton occupied the companion chair, wearing a matching dejected frown.

Wyatt's shoulders tensed. "Would you like a bite to eat before we go, Miss Cathryn?" His voice was as flat and lifeless as the empty fireplace he was staring into.

Milton exerted himself enough to chuckle. "Kitten, you are sunk. The use of your proper name does not bode well for your love match."

His movements sluggish as a drunk, Wyatt twisted toward Milton and pointed. "Knock it off. Your sister hates the name Kitten."

Milton blinked like a startled mouse. "I've always called her Kitten."

"You won't get your precious snuffbox back unless you do right by your sister," Wyatt growled the warning. "Find her a good husband. An honest gentleman with strong ties to the polo pony community."

Milton sank lower in the chair. "Right. Wouldn't want to have a vengeful cowboy plaguing my steps now, would I?"

Kitty planted herself in front of the fireplace. "I will not have my future discussed and decided as if I am a house plant or an heirloom ottoman with no opinions or feelings of my own."

His long legs unfolding like a stiff-limbed giraffe, Wyatt stood. Misery marred his handsome face. "I didn't mean to insult you. I want you to be happy and well loved."

Pain pulsed through her every fiber. With Wyatt she had both. "What about us?"

"He's throwing you over, Kitti—" Milton finished by clearing his throat.

"Leave!" Kitty and Wyatt said in unison.

Milton grunted with disgust, rose to his feet, and shuffled off to a back room.

Kitty stared into Wyatt's anguished eyes. Fear gnawed a hole in her heart. She loved Wyatt and had believed he loved. "I don't understand."

He held out his bandaged hands. "You heard my brothers. I mess up. All. The. Time. You saw for yourself. Someone could've gotten killed or hurt today because of me and my big mouth."

If anyone was to blame, it was Seth, but that was not an argument for this moment. She cradled Wyatt's injured hands. He was not a reckless goof-up. "Wyatt Haven, when I look at you I see a good and kind man who loves his family and would do anything for them."

Torment continued to contort his face. "That's why I have to leave them and you."

A ray of hope shone through the cracks in her heart. "But you wished we didn't have to divorce. Is that right?"

He wrapped her up in a tight embrace, holding her so close she could hear the thudding of his heart. "I never wanted anything as much as I want to be your husband. But if my stupidity got you—"

She captured his jaw. "Don't say that! You are not stupid."

He kissed her nose, reverting to playfulness, which didn't translate to his sad eyes. "I wouldn't dream of defying you."

She refused to be diverted. "Why do believe it's your responsibility to make everyone happy? I think there is more to your putting that snake in Levi's bed than meets the eye."

His brow furrowed. "I rescued the snake from Ma

Viola's cat. It was a harmless garden snake. Ace and Levi were sick with a fever. I thought seeing the snake would cheer them up. But the critter slithered out of my hands and landed on Levi's bed."

"And the butter churn. Why were you on the porch roof?"

Wyatt shrugged. "Ty and Boone were arguing, heading toward a fist fight."

Now that was a surprise. "But you and your brothers seem so close."

A hint of a smile puckered Wyatt's lips. "We are. But that don't make us saints."

Slightly disappointed to have her rosy picture of sibling bliss shattered, she circled back to her point. "So, you climbed on the porch roof and fell on the butter churn to stop the fight."

"I didn't see the butter churn until it was too late," he corrected.

He did it again—made her laugh when moments before she had felt close to tears. She kissed his cheek.

"What was that for?"

"For being you." She wrapped her arms around his square neck. "I know the truth. You do what you do to cheer up people."

His muscles tensed. "Nobody was laughing when Calvin died copying one of my dumb stunts."

Her frustration grew. "Hear me out. You hate to see others distressed or unhappy. That's why you joke and clown. When you rode with the Hole-in-the-Wall cattle rustlers you did it to survive."

He sighed, and rested his for head against hers. "That's a real nice thought, Kitty-Girl. But it don't change anything."

She was losing the argument. Losing him. "You are breaking my heart."

He set her at arm's length, his face pale and full of agony. "Trust me, you are safer without me." Then he turned and strode to the front door.

"There is a reason you are desperate to ensure everyone's happiness but your own," she called after him, as a frigid cold invaded her bones. "Promise me you will consider what I said."

He fled out the door without a backward glance.

He was slipping away from her.

"Do not need anyone," she whispered. "That's what Father would say."

She stood taller. "Horse hooey! I will not give up on us, Wyatt Haven. I will *not*."

Chapter Twenty-Eight

Kitty normally loved any excuse to ride, but between Wyatt's somber silence and Milton's grumbled complaints the half day journey to Aurora had been as bleak as the unrelenting drizzle oozing from the black clouds.

The walk from the livery stable to Johnson's Boardinghouse was equally grim.

Wyatt latched onto Milton's arm, keeping him from sneaking off. "You are not allowed out of my sight until after the trial tomorrow."

Milton bristled. "This is outrageous. You cannot hold me against my will."

"They don't call this the unlawful West for no reason," Wyatt said, dismissing the protest as if shooing away a pesky fly.

The shifty look in Milton's eyes said his only focus was on finding a means to escape back into his bad habits. "I will have an ally in Mother at least."

The familiar fatigue and weariness stemming from years of watching Milton's desultory descent into destructiveness, wrapped a smothering blanket around

Kitty's expectations. Once Wyatt gave up his vigil, her brother would likely return to his love affair with coca-laced snuff, and do it aided and abetted by their mother.

She entered the stuffy confines of the boardinghouse sitting room with a sense of dread. Wyatt's trial was looming. She wanted and needed time alone with him. Had he heeded her plea to examine his actions? Was he any closer to forgiving himself? Was he still determined to end their marriage?

Her feet halted at the sight of her mother seated on the blue-faded couch holding hands with a silver-haired gentleman. The man wore cowboy boots and a Western-style business suit. The radiant glow on her mother's face and new hairstyle made her look ten years younger.

Milton stared aghast. "Mother!"

"Children, I have wonderful news," Mother said, beaming. "This is Mr. Wilcox and we are to be married."

Kitty's mind spun dizzyingly. Mr. Wilcox had taken up residence at the boarding house the same day as Mother and Milton. Polite greetings had been exchanged. "Mother, we were away only two days. How is this even possible?"

Mother tranquilly fanned her face, filling the small space with the smell of her perfume. "After a mere hour in Mr. Wilcox's company I knew my life had changed forever."

Wyatt stood close to Kitty's elbow. She would never forget when he had stepped out of the crowd at the train station, a lasso twirling over his large white cowboy hat. The elegant ballet between man and horse, as he gently reeled in Lady Winsome.

The room now feeling roasting hot, Kitty wished she had a fan to cool her face. "May I suggest a longer engagement? It would allow you and Mr. Wilcox more time to get to know each other."

"But Kitty, how many times have you told me a new-born foal had the heart of a champion? That you positively knew the pony would be special." Mother smiled adoringly at Mr. Wilcox. "Sometimes you just know."

Mr. Wilcox was all gallantry as he kissed Mother's hand. "Elaine and I agreed we are greedy for all the happiness possible on the short trail of years remaining for us."

Mother giggled like a school girl.

London Bridge, the past several minutes were beyond surreal. Though pleased for her mother, Kitty couldn't help but be embarrassed by the gushy display between the lovey-dovey pair.

Wyatt tipped his cowboy hat. "That's right nice news. Congratulations."

Shaking off her shock, Kitty summoned up her warmest smile. Who was she to criticize her mother's judgment when she'd run away with a cattle rustler? Her trust had been based on nothing more than his friendly smile and his kindness to her ponies. "Congratulations. I wish you both all joy."

"Rubbish," Milton said, armed with the dignified bearing of an Englishman. "For all we know this man could be a swindler."

Mr. Wilcox was all brash American as he stood and

offered his hand to Milton. "Don't worry yourself over your mother. She'll enjoy every comfort. I own a mansion in Cheyenne and a three-thousand-acre cattle operation, west of the Haven spread. Wyatt can vouch for my good reputation."

Milton snubbed Mr. Wilcox's offered hand, in favor of reaching for his steel snuffbox. "You want a cattle rustler to vouch for you? How droll."

Wyatt ignored the insult. "Me and my family ain't fond of cattle barons, but John has always done right by us. Most folks in Aurora and Cheyenne would say that same."

Kitty bit back a giggle. Mrs. Elaine Cliffton was marrying a cattle baron. The gossips in London and Somerset were going to be in a flutter for weeks over this gem. Confident in Wyatt's judgment, she offered Mr. Wilcox a heartfelt smile as he helped Mother to stand. "I am sure you will make Mother wonderfully happy."

The thought her mother would be neighbors to the Havens jolted. "I hope you prepare Mother for the remoteness of your ranch."

"The ranch is only one of my business concerns," Mr. Wilcox explained, a winning twinkle in his eyes. "I employ a ranch foreman to oversee the day-to-day operations. Your mother and I will spend all of our time in Cheyenne or traveling."

Her fan fluttering like the graceful wings of a butterfly, Mother stared adoringly at Mr. Wilcox. "We plan to honeymoon in Europe."

"Mother, stop this ridiculousness," Milton demanded impatiently. "Send Kitty to purchase two train tickets for

New York City. As soon as the trial is over, we will leave this barbaric wilderness for good."

Mother frowned. "I was hoping you would stay for the wedding. But if you must go—"

"You are abandoning me?" A mix of disbelief and panic filled Milton's voice.

"You are a grown man," Mother said. "And well able to look after yourself."

The dismissive tone was a familiar one to Kitty. That it was directed at Milton came as a shock.

Milton stared as though poleaxed. "But I am not well. I need my medicine. My head aches. And I have the chills, and my stomach is—"

Mother clicked the fan closed. "Mr. Wilcox and I have dinner plans. You will have to ask Kitty to go the druggist and train station."

"Kitty cares only about her ponies," Milton said, pleading his case. "She will never agree to go to New York, even though her marriage to her dandy-doodle cowboy is a failure."

Kitty's face heated. Wearing a strained look, Wyatt shuffled in place.

Mother looped her arm with Mr. Wilcox's and gave Kitty a pitying look. "I warned your father it was not good for you to spend all your time with horses. Of course, you will be perfectly happy to be an old maid as long as you have your ponies."

"Who gives two fiddlesticks about Kitty?" Milton's snapped. "I am your darling boy. You cannot desert me."

Mother rolled her eyes. "Milton, do try to be less

dramatic."

Milton stared gape-mouthed.

"Do not wait up for me, children." Mother sailed out of the sitting room without a backward glance.

Kitty was equally jarred. *My ponies are all I need to be happy.* How many times had she repeated the belief? It wasn't true. Not anymore.

A ghost of a man, Milton slumped. "Where do we go from here, Kitten?"

She circled an arm around her brother's sloped shoulders. "Where do you want to go from here, Milton? What do you want to do with your life?"

Wyatt stood at the window with his back to her, seeming to be lost in his own thoughts.

Kitty knew her answer. "I want to be married to Wyatt," she whispered.

Milton made a sour face. "What makes you think Wyatt wants to be married to a woman who would choose her ponies over her husband?"

Her stomach twisted. "That is not fair."

"Blackwell tried to bargain, and you picked Lady Winsome. What was Wyatt supposed to think?" Milton shrugged. "Mother made her choice. Make yours."

"Choose?" Kitty swallowed heavily. She walked as in a daze to the door. "Excuse me."

And she fled into the dark.

Chapter Twenty-Nine

Wyatt whipped around at the sound of the boarding house door thudding shut. He was restless as a caged mountain lion in the stifling hot room. He narrowed his eyes at Cliffton. "What did you say to your sister to make her leave so suddenly?"

"Kitty could not care less about Mother running off with that cattle baron," Cliffton growled irritably. "Nobody cares about my suffering."

Wyatt held onto his patience. "Doc Craig said the next few days of your recovery would be the worst."

His clothes floating over his skeletal body, Cliffton paced the room, strangling the steel can. "Why do you care?"

"I'm not going to lie." Wyatt closed the distance between them. "You aren't the most likable fellow. But you are Kitty's brother and it pains her to see you wasting your life."

Cliffton grimaced. "Maybe I am happy wasting my life."

Wyatt doubted his words would reach the man's heart,

if he even had a heart, but he had to try. "Would you have sold Kitty's ponies to Blackwell without the coca snuff clouding your judgment?"

Cliffton stumbled to a halt. His voice rang with defensiveness. "The ponies' noses were dripping. It could have been equine influenza."

"Lady Winsome and the other ponies were and are in perfect health."

Cliffton massaged his temples. "You and Kitty and your infernal questions have given me a massive headache. Your moping is not helping. Do something silly to make me smile. Share a joke or an irreverent quip or a stupid story. Anything to make me laugh. You are supposed to be good at that."

Wyatt winced. The snide remark yanked a painful memory to the surface. But it was his father's desperate voice he heard. Wyatt was kneeling over his dying mother as their covered wagon rolled mile after mile over the Oregon Trail. *Son, make your mom smile.* Heeding his father's plea, Wyatt had done all he could to cheer his mother until she was buried at a nameless spot in the heart of Nebraska's endless prairies.

In her final pain-riddled moments his mother made Wyatt promise he would help his father to laugh again. *I always loved your father's laugh.* Those were her last words. One month later Wyatt's father was laid to rest in Wyoming after being trapped and crushed under the wheel of their wagon. Everyone tried to reassure Wyatt the accident wasn't his fault. Distracted by the joke Wyatt was telling, his father had failed to notice the brake slip free and the wagon rolling backward.

Fourteen years old and awash in guilt and pain, Wyatt had wandered aimlessly until his fateful encounter with Red Calder.

Cliffton was snapping his fingers close to Wyatt's face. "Hello. Is anyone home?"

Wyatt pushed his hand aside. "Where did Kitty go?"

Breaking it off with Kitty and leaving his family would have been the second huge mistake of his life. The first was hooking up with Red Calder's gang.

Wyatt hadn't told Kitty he loved her. A failure he intended to fix.

Chapter Thirty

A lone lantern cast shadows over Lady Winsome and Charger and the other horses stabled in the small livery barn. The soft nickering sounds and the smell of clean hay and fresh oats normally soothed Kitty, but Milton's accusation had jangled her nerves.

What makes you think Wyatt wants to be married to a woman who would choose her ponies over her husband?

"Hello, beautiful girl," she cooed, entering Winnie's stable box.

Winnie rubbed her head against Kitty's arm and neck.

The affectionate welcome brought stinging tears. She hugged Winnie and pressed her cheek to the pony's silky neck. "A mean man wants to punish me for embarrassing him. He says I must give you back. But I will not give you to Beau Blackwell. Not ever."

Blackwell's measures for dealing with spirited horses included the use of harsh words and whips. And the ranch foreman Amos Little had spoken of a glue factory.

She stroked Winnie's sleek chestnut coat and stared into her keen eyes. "But I cannot keep you, my sweet,

sweet girl. You see, I love Wyatt and I cannot allow him to hang or go to jail if I can save him by giving you up."

The pony's muzzle gently brushed her face and nuzzled her ear. Her tears increased at her dear, dear pony seeking to comfort her. "I promise you will go to someone who will take good care of you." She was prepared to shame Blackwell into agreeing to a proposal that Lady Winsome go to a third party. It was the only acceptable solution.

She leaned heavily against Winnie's flank. "I have come to say goodbye in private. I don't want Wyatt to see me cry or to believe I love you more than him."

"Whoa doggie, did I hear right?" Wyatt's soft drawl was the loveliest of music. "Did you say you love that rascal Wyatt Haven?"

Emotion clogged her throat. She nodded and brushed at the tears streaming down her cheeks. "You were not supposed to hear that."

His massive build ought to overwhelm the small confines of the stall, but he was all lazy grace as he entered the stable box. He rubbed Winnie's forehead and ears. "I don't mind sharing Miss Cathryn's love. How about you?"

Winnie replied by exhaling contented puffs of air.

He smiled. "Now if you'll excuse me, Lady Winsome, I have some serious wooing to attend to." His eyes brilliant as a summer sky, he gathered Kitty into his arms. "I know for a fact, the lady we adore has a big heart, with room enough to love us both."

She hugged him, thoroughly charmed over his including Winnie in the conversation. "Thank you."

He chuckled. "For what?"

She traced the lines of his chiseled jaw and strong cheekbones. Did he know what a change he had wrought in her heart and her life? "If you hadn't stepped into my life that day at the train station I might never have known true happiness. I love you, Wyatt Haven."

His face lit up. "Say that last part again, pretty please."

Joy bubbled up, and she gave him a smacking kiss. "I love you!"

Winnie neighed and bobbed her head.

He spun Kitty in a circle. "I love you, Kitty-Girl."

She laughed in delight. "Does that mean you want to make this a real marriage?"

He pulled back and stared soberly. "You were right about why I joke and jest."

She ran her hands over his strong back. "Tell me."

He poured out his heart, confiding all the painful details of his parents' deaths. She wept for his trials and sorrows and lost youth.

He finished with a heavy exhale. "I see now that putting myself down with names like numskull and fool doesn't honor my ma and daddy's memory."

She rested her head against his chest. "My father would not want me to give in to Mr. Blackwell's bullying. He'd say, horse hooey."

Wyatt kissed her forehead. "What would he say about you marrying a poor cowboy?"

She smiled. Horse hooey would have been his mildest response. "Father encouraged me to be independent and to chase my dreams. He never minded that I eschewed dances and pretty clothes in favor of days spent in horse barns and on the polo fields."

"He sounds like a sensible man. I'm surprised he didn't leave the ponies to you."

She sighed. "He promised they would be mine, but he never changed his will."

They held each other in silence, the moonlight streaming through the dusty barn window adding to the tranquility.

Wyatt spoke first. "About the trial."

"I'm going to accept Mr. Blackwell's bargain." She explained her plan to sell Lady Winsome to a third party.

Hearing her name, Winnie brushed against them.

Wyatt patted Winnie. "Let's hope it don't come to that."

"But it might."

He winked. "Blackwell best not be counting his chickens before they hatch. Frontier justice follows its own code."

She bit her lip. "He will be furious if you go free."

"Wouldn't be the first time." His smile faded. "Of course, with Blackwell's bad ticker, I'll have to be on my best behavior. Wouldn't want to have his heart fail him because of my saying or doing something dumb." He covered his mouth. "There I go again, besmirching my folks' memory."

She cupped his beautiful face. If she was worried about anyone's behavior at the trial, it was her brother's. Milton didn't care who he upset or hurt. "I wish Milton possessed a thimble worth of your goodness."

He pulled her close and kissed her soundly. Releasing

her, he frowned. "I left Milton in Boone's care, and it's a good bet one of them needs rescuing by now."

"I am sorry he has been a burden."

Wyatt shrugged. "It was my decision to prevent Milton from indulging his habit for coca snuff. After he testifies, I'll have to turn him over to his own devices."

She nodded, but she was too worried about the outcome of the trial to spare concern for anything else.

Chapter Thirty-One

By high noon the one-room schoolhouse turned temporary courtroom buzzed with anticipation. Wyatt was proud to have Kitty by his side, dressed in emerald-green and looking pretty as a spring bloom.

Kitty halted as they stepped over the threshold. "What is she doing here?"

He located the source of her surprise. Blond Tammy, of rhinestone purse fame, was snuggled up next to Beau Blackwell on the front bench. The pair glared back triumphantly.

Determined not say or do anything to rile Blackwell, Wyatt pasted on a smile and tipped his white Stetson. "Blackwell is trying to make you jealous."

Kitty made a face. "Tammy has my sympathy and is welcome to keep her *prize*."

He chuckled. "Do you mean to say, you're happy with your cowboy husband?"

Her smile was beautiful. "I hope to show you very soon how delighted I am with our marriage."

His step stuttered. "Some might say it was inviting bad

luck to speak of the future with the verdict of the trial still in doubt," he said for her ears only.

She held his hand more tightly. "Blame my future sisters-in-law." Her laugh was a nervous one. "I guess they already are my sisters-in-law. They were bubbling over with joy for you. For us. And planning a wedding dinner."

Half the audience was comprised of Havens.

When they reached Ty and Ella's bench, Ty gave Wyatt's arm a reassuring squeeze. "The whole family is rooting for you."

Ox, Levi, Ace turned in their seats and smiled.

"Whoa doggie," Wyatt said. "I thought you and the rest of the boys would still be up at the north pasture mending the fence and rounding up the herd."

Beefy face red and shining, Ox stabbed his thumb over his shoulder. "Seth and Wally rounded up all the small nesters to finish the job. Ugly Sally and Buck stayed to supervise the work. They send their best."

"That was right good of Seth," Wyatt said, surprised but warmed by the gesture.

Ox nodded. "Seth made the suggestion and volunteered to go."

Kitty hugged his arm. "Seth wants to make peace."

"I hope you're right." Wyatt spotted Seth, Wally, and White Wolf standing along the back wall of the packed schoolhouse. As usual, Wally jabbered away at Seth and White Wolf while they were scanning the room for trouble.

Wyatt was humbled. "It sure is good to have the whole family here."

A few steps more brought Wyatt and Kitty to Levi and Ace's bench.

Ace's eyes twinkled with mischief. "Let's get this show on the road. Some of us have places to be."

Levi's jaw clenched. "Ace is itching to set eyes on the Jewel of Texas."

"Levi's just jealous that Jewel favors me," Ace crowed.

Levi scoffed. "I'd like to know why the lady gambler joined forces with Blackwell. Why Aurora? Cheyenne is where the real money is."

"Don't make sense, does it?" Wyatt agreed.

Ace rubbed his hands with relish. "It sure will be fun trying the learn Jewel's secrets."

Levi snorted. "Blackwell will grow angel wings before Jewel confides in you."

Kitty grinned at their show. "Mr. Ace, I think you might be more of a rogue than Wyatt."

Ace got a hoot out of that. "Plain old Ace will do."

Levi jabbed Ace. "Wyatt's bride has got you figured out."

Amusement dancing in her eyes, Kitty pulled Wyatt along to the next row, where Garrett and his plucky Swedish bride Brigetta were riding herd on Billy, Juan, and Tucker.

"Win, win, win," the boys chanted, reaching over each other to give Wyatt a slap of support.

Garrett mussed Tucker's hair. "Root beers all around after Judge Peck says Mr. Wyatt didn't do nothing wrong."

Wyatt danced in place and shadow punched the air. "I might even have me a root beer float."

The boys copied him, batting the air with their fists.

Kitty curled her lips inward as if to prevent a smile.

"Settle down," Wyatt cautioned. "You'll be getting me in hot water with Miss Brigetta."

Brigetta's crown of blond braids shined gloriously. "Ja, but it is a good for you that you are my favorite devil."

Wyatt winked. "And I'm twice as handsome as Garrett."

Brigetta flapped her hand. "He is a handful." The comment was directed at Kitty. "But he has a heart of gold."

Kitty pushed closer. "You are quite right, Brigetta. And I would not have it any other way."

Brigetta nodded her approval.

"No teaming up to make me blush," Wyatt drawled, tickled to see Kitty and his family hitting it off so well.

He drew Kitty ahead to the next bench and greeted Boone, his wife Maggie, and their four-year son old Colt.

"I hope to get your schoolhouse back to you real quick, Miss Maggie," Wyatt said.

Colt tipped back his head and grinned ear to ear. "Did you hear? Mama is having a baby."

Her face radiant, Maggie hugged Colt. "Hush, my love."

Wyatt squeezed Boone's shoulder. "Congratulations, *daddy*."

Boone's star-pinned chest swelled. "Maggie and Ella have some party planned for you two."

Wyatt suffered a moment of doubt. "If the trial doesn't go well…" Sheriff Boone would be responsible for carrying out the hanging, if it came to that. Boone would refuse, and Blackwell would undoubtedly volunteer his men to carry out the unpleasant task.

"Don't go there," Boone said reading his mind. "At the worst, the judge will order you to give the horses back to Blackwell and send you to jail for a few months."

Wyatt felt Kitty's tremble against his arm. "I should be the one on trial."

"Shh," he whispered, pressing a kiss the side of her face. "This isn't about the ponies."

Tammy's sharp voice echoed through the schoolhouse. "Some people have no class." She nudged Blackwell. "Ain't that right, honey?"

Blackwell's rat-colored mustache drooped lower. "Wyatt Haven has a bad habit of making public scenes."

Wyatt's spine stiffened. Lassoing Blackwell at the Double B rodeo had earned him a black mark. Wrapping the man in a tablecloth and throwing him over his shoulder like a sack of potatoes had been the death kiss.

"If anyone should be outraged by the newspaper picture it's me," Kitty whispered back. "Well, here is a picture Mr. Blackwell will not forget." Then his proper English bride stood on her tiptoes and kissed the daylights out of him.

Cheers and whoops of delight rang out.

Wyatt hugged her tight. "Hoo wee, what was that about?"

A hint of pink tinged her ivory complexion. Head held high, she stared defiantly at Blackwell and Tammy. "Wyatt and I are husband and wife. Nothing could make me prouder or happier than being Mrs. Wyatt Haven."

Blackwell's jowls sagged lower. "You are a disappointment, woman."

"You will recover, Mr. Blackwell." Her clipped British accent substituted for a slap to the face. "I did."

Tammy pouted. "You can do better than her."

"Button it," Blackwell growled, swiveling back around.

Heart bursting with love and pride for his family and his bride, Wyatt steered Kitty toward Mrs. Elaine Cliffton. The grand lady looked a queen deposited among mere peasants.

"I am still in shock over Mother's Mr. Wilcox offering to stand as your lawyer," Kitty said. "I am sure it will help."

"Let's hope he's a better lawyer than a cattleman."

Six years ago, Mr. Wilcox was a highfalutin Boston lawyer. Beau Blackwell used to be a New York banker. Rich city fellows and British and Scottish lords who didn't know the first thing about proper management of cattle operation buying their way into the cattle business were partly responsible for the collapsing markets that had everyone on edge.

"Look who is here," Kitty exclaimed, spotting Henrietta and Theodore Rochester sitting on the other side of her mother.

"Howdy," Wyatt said, returning the couple's smiles. "It's mighty good of you to be here for Kitty."

A dynamo of a woman, Henrietta bristled with energy even though not in motion. "Theodore and I came to support both you and Kitty."

"Hen and I think you're a good chap," Theodore added.

Mrs. Cliffton swiped the air with her hideous yellow fan. "Henrietta and Theodore, stop chitchatting and allow Wyatt to take his seat at the defense table with Mr. Wilcox."

Wyatt wagged his brows. "We best listen to Mrs. Cliffton. She's in a hurry to marry Mr. Wilcox, who's plumb delighted to have won her favor."

The lady in question couldn't have looked more pleased as Kitty took her seat. Wyatt felt better about leaving her behind, knowing she would enjoy Henrietta and Theodore's full care.

He dropped down on the wooden chair set behind a plain oak table.

Mr. Wilcox pushed a piece of paper in front of him. "Peruse the witness list and tell me if any of the names jump out at you."

The next instant a side door opened, and the witnesses filed in.

Cliffton avoided Wyatt's eyes as he trudged to the reserved seating. He carried a small satchel. In the last words they'd shared, Wyatt had encouraged Cliffton to speak the truth. He'd considered asking him not to make up lies, but wouldn't put it past his brother-in-law to lie just to be spiteful.

The other witnesses, most being Blackwell's ranch hands, took their seats. Then the Jewel of Texas floated into the room like a wavering desert mirage.

Gasps resounded.

Wyatt hadn't recovered from this shock, when Jed

Daltrey sauntered through the door wearing the signature Daltrey Gang light blue bandanna.

Wyatt's muscles tightened. He didn't have to see his brothers to know they'd likewise gone on full alert.

Mr. Wilcox tapped the witness list. "I almost refused Jewel and Jed as character witnesses. But then I thought, why not. Having a cardsharp and bank robber as character witnesses could work to our advantage."

Wyatt rubbed his eyes, unsure he was reading right. But there it was in black and white. The Jewel of Texas and Jed Daltrey listed as witnesses for the defense.

Beau Blackwell jumped to his feet and pointed an accusing finger at Wyatt. "What's the meaning of this?"

Wyatt shrugged. "Darned if I know."

Chapter Thirty-Two

Kitty's ears rang with the uproar caused by the surprise witnesses. Before she had time to recover from this shock, Henrietta and Theodore scooted over, making room for White Wolf.

He settled beside Kitty, his long hair pooled on the bench and a hint of a smile showing. "I bet you're wondering what Jewel and Jed Daltrey are doing here?"

The directness of the Haven men took getting used to. "Hello to you too," she replied softly.

Her mother grasped her arm. "Cathryn, who, who, who—"

"Mr. White Wolf is Wyatt's brother," Kitty explained in a rush.

Henrietta and Theodore, who knew White Wolf from his visit to Rosewood Ranch, took his presence in stride.

But Mother looked ready to faint. "Oh my. What does he—"

"We will talk later, Mother," Kitty said, cutting off the rude comments sure to follow.

White Wolf didn't spare her mother a look. "You

probably noticed folks take a real liking Wyatt?"

"Everyone but Mr. Blackwell and Tammy," Kitty said.

White Wolf chuckled. "You and Wyatt are going to be good together. Your children will be strong of mind and heart."

Her staid British sensibilities rattled, her face heated. "I believe you are right, Mr. Wo…" She stammered to a stop. "What should I call you?"

He tipped his head. "I go by Wolf."

By marrying Wyatt, she was gaining a large interesting family bound by tremendous love and respect. Eager to embrace and explore this fresh new start with Wyatt, she welcomed any help that would get them over the hurdle of the trial. "Wolf, please tell me Jewel's and Jed's testimonies will help Wyatt."

Though speaking affably, White Wolf remained watchful. "I heard the pair were going out of their way to speak good of Wyatt. Funny thing is, their word carries weight, exactly because they come from the wrong side of the law."

"It takes a criminal to know a criminal?" she suggested, her gaze turning to Milton. Seated across the aisle, her brother sat bent over with his face in his hands. It would be nice to think he was miserable over the trouble he had started by selling her ponies to Mr. Blackwell. But she resigned herself to the fact, he was probably feeling sorry for himself, or counting the seconds until he could indulge in his *medicine*.

"People can surprise you," Wolf said, reclaiming her attention. "I told Jewel and Jed if they really wanted to help Wyatt they should step forward. And they did."

She placed her hand on Wolf's copper-colored one. "I am sure it will work. Thank you."

His words continued to resound. *People can surprise you.* Mother's engagement to Mr. Wilcox had come as a monumental shock. And who would have believed Miss Cathryn Cliffton would marry a cattle rustler? If she and Mother could make such a dramatic change to their chosen paths, perhaps Milton could too.

"Thank you," she repeated, taking hold of the slim hope.

Wolf squeezed her fingers. "Wyatt deserves most of the credit. He has the gift for making people laugh and feel good. Just watch, and you'll see him work his magic on the jury and Judge Peck."

Wyatt was putting his angelic charm to use on Mr. Wilcox, who was smiling and laughing as they chatted. Wyatt would be embarrassed to hear White Wolf's praise. He would protest, saying he didn't deserve credit for acting foolish. His humility added to his electric attractiveness.

As if sensing her watching, Wyatt turned to her. Love shone in his blue eyes.

She forced a smile, not wanting him to be distracted by worry for her.

The side door opened, and the jury shuffled to their assigned seats in front of the black chalkboard.

Holding her breath, Kitty turned to White Wolf. "Did we get a good jury?"

He crossed his buckskin-clad arms. "We got Doc Craig

and Gary Tyler of Tyler's Seed and Grain and the foreman from the Crooked J who isn't on friendly terms with Blackwell. There's some cowboys and smaller nesters who know Wyatt from way back. We're doing good. Very good."

The jurors sat except for an elderly, stoop-shouldered man. He squinted in Wyatt's direction. "Is that you, Wyatt?"

"Yes, Sir, Mr. Baker," Wyatt answered with good humor, waving his arms.

Mr. Baker held up a slip of paper. "If'n we vote to hang you, don't be forgetting the five dollars you owe me for the tea towels and other niceties you ordered for the new missus."

Everyone laughed, including Wyatt. "I promise. Personally, I'm hoping to do business with the Last Chance Trading Post for many, many more years."

Mr. Baker slid the receipt into his pocket, sat, and whispered loudly to the person next to him. "I think Wyatt's innocent. What about you?"

"Who asked you, Ned?" Beau Blackwell growled.

Ned Baker's face screwed up. "You did. When you came by the trading post hoping to intimidate me. The way I see it, Wyatt and the Havens are decent folks who deserve a fair shake."

The other jurors nodded in agreement as snickers echoed through the schoolhouse.

The puffy bags under Blackwell's eyes made him look old rather than sinister. "That just proves you small nesters are too stupid for your own good."

Tammy fluffed her blond hair. "You tell him, honey."

Wyatt smiled amiably. "I'd say us small nesters have gumption. We'll be here long after you cattle barons skedaddle to greener pastures."

A chill shiver went through Kitty at how close she had come to disaster. If she had not run away, she would be Mrs. Blackwell rather than Mrs. Haven.

Kitty would be eternally thankful she had heeded her heart and put her trust in a golden-haired, blue-eyed cattle rustler.

Judge Peck and the prosecuting attorney and the bailiff entered, guffawing over a private joke. The judge ensconced himself behind the schoolteacher's desk.

Wolf leaned closer. "The judge, prosecutor, and bailiff travel the circuit courts together. You can bet they've already talked about the case and have their minds made up to the outcome."

She prayed he was correct. Her brief moments in the judge's company when he had married her and Wyatt left her with a good impression. And Wyatt and his brothers were pleased Judge Peck was presiding over the trial. But she still felt uneasy. "That is an eyebrow-raising system."

A shadow crossed Wolf's face. "It's called frontier justice. Sometimes it helps and other times it hurts."

Though fascinated by the West and well on her way to loving it, she couldn't deny the darker aspects. If Blackwell's heart had not failed, he and his posse might have dispensed justice by hanging Wyatt without the benefit of a trial.

Judge Peck pounded a gavel, and a hush descended in

the schoolroom. The portly man folded his arms over a black robe stained with evidence of a recent meal and rested his weight on the desk. "Happily for me, this ought to be quick. We're headed to Buffalo next for a circus-like trial of two bigamists. Seems the cowboy and prostitute in question already had three or four spouses each before tying the knot. Folks will be flocking from miles around to hear the salacious details."

Judge Peck riffled a pile of documents. "Do we have a Mr. Milton Cliffton in attendance?"

Milton slowly climbed to his feet. Between his sunken cheeks and the Savile Row suit sagging on his wasted body, he appeared far older than his twenty-four years. "Unfortunately, that would be me."

Wire-rimmed spectacles perched on the end of his bulbous nose, Judge Peck studied Milton like a bug under a glass. "Did you send a note to the prosecutor with pivotal information?"

Kitty's pulse kicked. London Bridge! What new mischief was Milton up to?

Wyatt glanced over his shoulder and winked, offering her silent reassurance.

She managed a shaky smile, determined to be equally brave.

Milton fished the metal snuffbox from a breast pocket. "Of course, I wrote the letter. Did you think it came from Queen Victoria?"

Judge Peck's face puckered. "Don't get snippy with me, Mr. Cliffton."

Milton winced. "You will have to excuse me, as I have

a deuced headache. May I make my statement and go? I am most eager to crawl into a dark hole."

"Yes, yes," Judge Peck said irritably. "Right after you are sworn in. But be warned, if you persist with the rude remarks, I will instruct the bailiff to arrest for contempt of court."

After taking his place at the witness table and swearing to tell the truth, Milton exhaled wearily and gazed at the snuffbox. "Wyatt Haven is completely innocent."

Beau Blackwell shot to his feet. "Don't be ridiculous."

"I would take offense, but it requires too much energy," Milton replied dryly.

"Get on with matters," Judge Peck ordered.

Milton's eyes went back to Wyatt. "My sister is, and was, the legal owner of the ponies. So you are guilty of nothing."

Beau Blackwell's brow creased. "What's this nonsense, Cliffton? You sold the horses to me."

"My father left the ponies to my sister in his will," Milton confessed, massaging his temple. "I lied to you and to her."

Disbelief and anger warred for supremacy on Beau Blackwell's face "I'll want to see proof, you miserable liar."

Milton pocketed the snuffbox and hoisted his small satchel. "You and Judge Peck are welcome to inspect my father's will at your leisure."

The schoolhouse erupted in noisy chatter.

The rat-a-tat of Judge Peck's gavel rang out. "Case dismissed."

Head down, Milton tried to make an escape.

Shaking in disbelief and shock, Kitty found her voice. "Why, Milton? Why all the lies?"

Milton paused beside her bench. Eyes that were usually drug-hazed had cleared. "I resented you because you were Father's favorite."

"But you loved me best," Mother said, indignant.

Milton didn't heed the rebuke. "If only I could have been good and dutiful like you."

Kitty twisted her hands together. How different everything would have been if they had been the best of friends instead of rivals. "I was a disappointment to Father too. Because I wasn't a boy."

Milton shrugged. "Father threatened to leave everything to you if I did not mend my ways."

"My ponies were the only thing I wanted."

Milton's gaunt face was tragically sad. "I suppose I sold your ponies to Blackwell to punish you. That was rather hateful."

The pitiful olive branch was a start. Kitty touched his sleeve. "But in the end, you told the truth."

"Kitty," Wyatt called over the heads of the people thronging around him and offering congratulations.

Milton cocked his head. "Your cowboy husband deserves the gratitude."

She waved at Wyatt. Tall, blond, and wide-shouldered, he was the gentlest of giants. Who would have believed an heiress from Somerset and a reformed cattle rustler would marry and fall in love? Not her.

Her brother shuffled away, joining the bodies clogging

the center aisle.

Wyatt took the direct route, hopping over the benches separating them and caught her up in his arms. "Your ponies are safe, Kitty-Girl. Even Lady Winsome."

Mother wore a horrified look. "Mr. Haven, show some decorum."

"Horse hooey," Kitty said, hugging him tight. "You are perfect. Don't change, ever."

Wyatt's grin was mischievous. "Do you want to bust out of here and go tell Lady Winsome the good news?"

"Nothing would make me happier."

"You got it, pretty lady," Wyatt said, and scooped her up and headed for the back door.

Mother gasped, positively scandalized.

But Kitty was not a bit embarrassed. Life with Wyatt would not be predictable or boring. And how lovely was that?

Chapter Thirty-Three

Wading through the folks congratulating him, Wyatt left behind the stuffy schoolhouse and carried Kitty down the steps. With the brilliant sunshine and warm spring breeze, it was as if the heavens were also offering them blessings.

His brothers crowded around, slapping him on the back and sharing in his happiness.

He set Kitty down so his sisters-in-law could hug her and tell her how happy they were for them.

Judge Peck paused in passing. His eyes held a twinkle. "I take it you two won't be needing a divorce?"

"No divorce," he and Kitty answered together to much laughter.

Judge Peck chuckled. "Congratulations, Mr. and Mrs. Haven."

Wyatt couldn't stop smiling as he watched the judge walk away. Their lickety-split marriage had been risky and maybe even a little reckless. But if he'd played it safe, he might've missed out on winning Kitty's love.

The milling crowd parted for the Jewel of Texas. Yellow dress and golden hair rivaling the sun for glory, her aloofness combined with great beauty had a tongue-tying effect on menfolk. She acknowledged Wyatt and Kitty with the tilt of the head as she sailed serenely in the direction of the Rawhide Saloon.

"White Wolf said Miss Jewel went out of her way to speak well of you," Kitty said, eying him curiously.

He winked. "Are you jealous?"

She blushed prettily. "Maybe."

He circled his arm at her waist. "The Jewel ain't my kind of woman."

Kitty smiled. "No?"

He hadn't ever seen anything more beautiful than Kitty riding her pony across an open field. "A horsey woman is more to my liking."

"And I love my kind husband." She pressed closer. "White Wolf said you have a gift for making people smile and feel good. And they, in return, will go out of their way to repay the kindness."

"You are some special yourself. Wolf usually ain't one for talking." Wyatt couldn't be more pleased. Any doubts over Miss Cathryn Cliffton not fitting in had vanished.

Jewel wanting to testify on his behalf still baffled. "I kind of wish the trial had lasted long enough to hear what Miss Jewel had to say. I played a few hands of poker at her table. None of what was said stands out, except Milton insulting her. And her threatening Milton with her small pistol after he stole her lucky gold coin."

Wyatt reached in his pocket and freed the gold coin he'd lifted from Milton when he took away the pilfered snuffbox. "Thunderation, I forgot to return Jewel's lucky coin."

Ace and Levi tripped over themselves to get to Wyatt.

Wagging his brows, Ace reached for the coin. "It just so happens, I've been itching to join a game at Miss Jewel's table. I'd be happy to do the honors."

Levi knocked Ace's hand aside. "Chasing after Miss Jewel will only land you in trouble." Turning to Wyatt, Levi held out his hand. "Give me the coin. That will save everyone a whole lot of aggravation."

"I didn't mean to cause a rift." Wyatt flipped the coin off his thumb.

Ace deftly snagged it and sauntered away. "Don't worry. Levi is a good loser."

Levi caught up to Ace and put a hitch in the other man's swagger by prying the coin out of his hand.

Wyatt laughed and shook his head. "Poor Levi. Keeping up with Ace is giving him gray hairs."

Kitty wore a thoughtful look. "Levi is partial to Miss Jewel."

"Levi and Jewel?" he said, astonished. "What makes you say that?"

"Women sense these things."

He shuddered at the thought. "That's not good." There would be plenty of fireworks if Levi and Ace tangled over the same woman. Nobody would win, except maybe the Jewel of Texas.

Milton drifted over, his color ghastly gray. "While we are on the subject of stolen property."

Wyatt felt Kitty tense. "The snuffbox does not belong to you," she said. We will be returning it to the queen's second cousin."

Wyatt fetched the fancy blue box from his shirt pocket. "Would you like to scratch out a letter of apology before we send it to London?"

Milton's gaze fixated on the snuffbox. His left cheek twitched. "How soon would you need such a document?"

Wyatt tucked away the snuffbox. "That depends on you. You can return to your destructive ways. Or you are welcome to spend time at Sweet Creek Ranch, regaining your strength and health."

Milton's haunted eyes slid to Kitty. "Would you welcome me, after what I have done?"

Her chin came up. "I can forgive the past. But I cannot and will not tolerate you indulging your coca snuff habit or substituting similar toxic *medicine*. Are you willing to accept those terms?"

Eyes darting, Milton fidgeted with the various pockets of his la-di-da suit. "You drive a hard bargain, Kitten…er…sister."

Mrs. Cliffton and Mr. Wilcox walked by with their heads together. Wyatt couldn't believe they would be so oblivious to Kitty and Milton.

Kitty rubbed her crossed arms. "America is a place for starting over."

Milton nodded. "A few weeks of mountain air might be what I need."

Kitty bit her lip. "Wyatt says there are dozens of splendid horse trails."

Milton's nose wrinkled. "The mere thought of bouncing over mountains on the back of a horse makes me ill. Which is fair, as ponies and horses do not have a high opinion of me either."

The tentative smile Kitty and Milton shared was a start. Past hurts would require time to heal. Establishing trust would take longer. They would be starting from scratch when it came to the love, respect, and support that was the mainstay of the Haven family. But they couldn't come to a better place than Sweet Creek Ranch to learn lessons on what it meant to be family. Wyatt would encourage them every step of the way.

The one o'clock train chugged into town, accompanied by several noisy blasts of the horn.

Jed Daltrey strutted up to them. "Red always said you were a lucky dog." The tanned wrinkles edging his green eyes punctuated his cocky grin. "You was saved from my fine speechifyin' on your behalf."

Wyatt had dodged a bullet on that count for sure. "It don't make sense. You wanting to help me."

Jed shrugged. "You was one of Red's boys."

Kitty squeezed Wyatt's arm. "Wyatt is a Haven. A second-chance boy."

Her feisty defense on his behalf was a fine sight to behold, but unnecessary. He knew what he was and what he wasn't. "I ran with cattle rustlers for a while after my ma and daddy died, but thankfully Pa Malcolm and Ma Viola rescued me. I am who I am because of them. Not Red. Not you."

Jed thought on that for a long moment. "Yep, you always were a lucky dog." Then he strolled away, whistling between his teeth.

Antsy for some private time with Kitty, Wyatt laced his fingers with hers, and strode for the stables located on the opposite corner.

Halfway across the mud-slicked road, a passel of riders charged toward them.

Beau Blackwell led the way, brandishing a horsewhip. Vengeance was written in his dark glower and snarling mouth.

Chapter Thirty-Four

They were trapped in the middle of the roadway with a dozen horses bearing down on them. No time to run, no place to hide. A single refrain looped through Wyatt's brain. *Protect Kitty. Protect Kitty.*

Mud splashed from hooves as the men encircled them. Blackwell pulled his gelding to a rearing halt, a leather whip gripped overhead.

Kitty lifted her arms in a protective effort. "No, no!"

Wyatt tugged her against his chest, turned his back to Blackwell, and curled into a ball to create as small a target as possible as the whip slashed through the air.

The leather cracked across his back, his buckskin jacket absorbing the worst of the impact. Kitty shrieked.

Wyatt's heart thundered, and he swiveled his head around. He glared at Blackwell. "You will pay dearly if you harm my wife."

The whip slashed downward.

Wyatt raised his arm and twisted away. The leather bit into his sleeve. The tail nicked his cheek.

"Stop hitting him!" Kitty cried.

Three blasts from a gun rang out, followed by Boone's commanding voice. "Drop the whip, Blackwell, or I'll drop you."

Wyatt chanced a look.

Blackwell's eyes locked with his as he slowly coiled the whip and his mount pranced nervously. "Who's the big shot now?"

Blood trickled from a stinging wound. Slowly becoming aware of dogs barking in the distance and the nervous milling of spectators, Wyatt couldn't make sense of Blackwell's words. "Big shot?"

Blackwell laughed grimly. "You thought it was real funny when you lassoed me. But you aren't laughing now, are you?"

Boone walked among the posse. "Get going before I arrest you."

Blackwell's men exchanged unsure looks.

Amos Little waved for the men to disperse. "The boss taught Wyatt a lesson."

The men backed their horses away, but didn't go far. Amos stayed put, wearing a smug smile.

Wyatt examined Kitty for injuries. "Did he hurt you?"

Tears slid down her face as she shook her head and touched her fingers to his face. "I am so sorry."

"It wasn't your fault." His voice was rough with emotion at the mere possibility of her being struck with the whip.

Drawing her tight to his side, he rested his free hand next to his gun and narrowed his eyes at Blackwell. "My lassoing you at the rodeo and tossing you over my shoulder at the Longhorn club was plumb foolish. I regret embarrassing you. Or I did."

Ty stepped out of the protective wall his brothers had formed acting as a barrier between the trouble and the woman and children and townsfolk. And an impressive force it was with Ty, White Wolf, Garrett, Ox, and Seth armed to the teeth and masked in fierce expressions.

The most level-headed of the lot, Ty simmered with anger. "The only harm Wyatt did was to your pride. Because people laughed. Do you see anyone laughing?"

Ashen-faced, Ella, Maggie, and Brigetta worked to calm the children with hugs and whispered words.

Old Ned Baker wore the look of disgust he aimed at cowboys who missed the spittoon stationed on the porch outside his store.

Deep frowns screwed up the faces of the assembled shopkeepers, cowboys, and farmers.

"Us cattle barons can't buy a fair trial with you small nesters," Blackwell growled. "So I wrangled up my own justice."

Wyatt clenched his jaw. "I'm guilty of plenty of stupid stunts, but I never hurt a person or animal on purpose. Whipping me was plain mean."

Murmurs of agreement swept through the crowd.

A colorful flush crept up Blackwell's neck. "You deserved it. Stealing my bride was a lowdown move."

Kitty's chin jutted, and she stood taller. "Wyatt did not steal me. He helped me to run away." Then she looked up at Wyatt with love shining in her eyes. "He could not have been more gallant, brave, and kind."

Blackwell sneered. "He's a dumb cowboy."

Tammy barged through the crowd. "He can't hold a candle to you."

Blackwell didn't spare her a glance. "I told you to get to the hotel room and stay there."

Tammy frowned. "I wanted to see Wyatt get licked for that humiliating picture in the *Daily News*."

"Button it, Tammy," Blackwell barked.

Kitty's composure didn't slip. "I am proud to be Mrs. Wyatt Haven. If I had made the mistake of marrying you, I could not say as much."

His face souring, Blackwell shifted on his saddle. "You're a disappointment, darling."

Wyatt's hands fisted. His easygoing nature had limits. "I'll kindly ask you not to speak disrespectful to my wife and to Miss Tammy."

Blackwell bristled. "Are you threatening me?"

Amos Little, who had been listening the whole time, smirked and leaned forward on his horse. "Sounds like you need another lesson in manners."

Tammy shook her bejeweled purse at Wyatt. "Whip him good this—"

A gunshot rang out. The bullet tore Tammy's purse from her hand. A scream ripped from her throat.

A few townsfolk rushed to her aid, as she crumpled into a puddle of frightened tears. She didn't appear to have suffered an injury.

Shielding Kitty and freeing his gun, Wyatt search for the source of the gun blast.

Blackwell's men had their guns trained on Wally.

Wreathed in smoke, the boy beamed in the direction of the men. "Told you I was as good a shot as Seth."

The second-chance boys stared back dumbfounded.

Wyatt sympathized with their plight. A kick from a bull would've been less of a jolt.

Blackwell swung down from his horse and advanced on Wally with the whip. "You little rat."

Wyatt, Ty, and Boone stepped in his path.

Hatred and anger flashed in his dark eyes. "You Havens think you can get away with anything."

Seth confiscated Wally's gun, marched him off to the side while chewing him out.

Blackwell pointed the whip at Wyatt. "Your kind is what ails the cattle business. And them brats you foster are an infection Aurora doesn't need."

Patience disintegrating, Wyatt took hold of the whip and employed his towering height and bulk to stare Blackwell into the ground.

Tammy, Amos, and Blackwell's men squawked complaints.

Wyatt silenced them with a look.

Satisfied he commanded everyone's attention, he released the whip. "It's greedy cattle barons like you overstocking and over-grazing the land that caused the collapse of the cattle business. The cattle drives and the open plains was special, but times have changed. Fences and small nesters are here to stay." He narrowed his eyes at Blackwell. "Get used to it or move on."

That got plenty of nods and grunts of agreement.

Wyatt draped his arms around Ty's and Boone's

shoulders. "The Havens will be here long after you're gone."

Claps and cheers erupted.

Blackwell stalked to his horse.

"Wait for me," Tammy called, hurrying after him.

Kitty rushed into Wyatt's arms.

His heart burst with joy as he gazed on the faces of family and friends. "Pa Malcolm and Ma Viola started something good. We promised Pa and Ma we'd carry on their work. And we will."

Amid a chorus of amens and calls of encouragement, Levi and Ace joined Ty and Boone, followed by White Wolf, Ox, and Garrett. The younger second-chance boys danced around them.

Ty squeezed his shoulder. "You done good, Wy. Pa and Ma would be proud."

"Not just with me," Wyatt said, immensely pleased by Ty's praise. "Pa and Ma would be happy seeing us sticking together and working together."

Smiles reigned, except on Seth. He led Wally forward, with a tight grip on his shirt collar. "Me and Wally got something to say."

Wally tucked his thumb in his pockets. "Holy moly, I don't know what the big deal is. I missed that Tammy lady by a mile."

Seth wore a guilt-ridden face. "Shooting that mug out of Wyatt's hand the other day was stupid and reckless."

A gunslinger in the making, Seth was a crack shot and could easily have inflicted damage if that had been his intent. Wyatt hadn't been in any real danger. They both knew that.

Seth stared down at the muddy ground. "I've mean-talked you for what happened with Calvin. Now I'm the one who messed up."

Wyatt understood the pain of letting his brothers and family down. "We all mess up."

Seth was driven by the hostility and cynicism he wore on his sleeve. His attitude could easily get someone hurt or killed. Especially if he continued on his present path. Wyatt held out his hand, to shake hands man to man. "The past can't be undone. But you can learn from it."

Wally stuck out his hand. "I'll shake your hand, Mr. Wyatt. You said I'd feel at home at Sweet Creek Ranch."

Wyatt shook the pudgy hand and ruffled Wally's hair. "What do you like best?"

Wally smiled. "It's been splendiferous fun riding horses and roping and doing all that other cowboy stuff."

"Whoa doggie," Wyatt said. "Are you sure you're old enough to be slinging those five-dollar words?"

Wally and the other second-chance boys laughed uproariously.

Even Seth smiled.

Wyatt offered Seth his hand again. "Brothers through thick and thin. That's what Pa and Ma wanted for us."

Eyes swimming, Seth clasped his hand. "Brothers to the end."

Seth didn't resist when Wyatt pulled him in for a bear hug. Family and home was and would always be Wyatt's greatest happiness. "It's good to be home, brother. It's good to be home."

Chapter Thirty-Five

Ty and Ella couldn't have given Wyatt a better wedding present than a night alone at Sweet Creek Ranch with Kitty. The soft glow of lamplight on the pine floors. The crackling fire in the floor-to-ceiling fireplace. The faint smell of cinnamon.

In the aftermath of yesterday's trial, an awkward discussion had arisen as to where he and Kitty would spend their first night as true husband and wife.

Kitty bravely suggested one of the saloons, which he immediately ruled out. He might not be able to offer Miss Cathryn Cliffton silk sheets, but he wouldn't subject her to the sights, sounds, and smells of a saloon hotel room. Kitty's mother and brother occupied the boardinghouse, ruining the most suitable option.

Wyatt wanted to kiss Ty and Ella when they insisted on staying an extra night at Maggie and Boone's place. They arranged for the second-chance boys to bunk at Garrett and Brigetta's small ranch.

Amid the unusual stillness, he was aware of each heartbeat as he waited for Kitty to emerge from his bedroom. *Their* bedroom. Too restless to sit, he wandered back to the fireplace and admired the glass jelly-jar half full of shiny red, blue, green, and yellow marbles.

He retrieved the burlap bag from his pocket and emptied the contents into his palm.

Thanks to Kitty pointing out his need to make folks smile, he'd found a measure of peace. Running away wouldn't bring Calvin back. The best way to honor his folks' and Calvin's memory was to love his family with every inch of his heart and continue to spread joy and laughter where he could.

He stroked the warm glass, and dropped Red's silver bullet and the last of Calvin's marbles into the jelly jar. "Brothers forever. You will always be in my heart."

Replacing the picture of his folks in the burlap sack and carefully tucking it away, he roamed to the pine table, where the family shared noisy, lively meals. Until Kitty came along, he'd been rootless and adrift. Talk of becoming a chili chef, champion rodeo rider, blacksmith, trick rider had been hogwash.

The cowboy life had always suited him. Until now, nothing would have pleased him more than to remain at Sweet Creek Ranch for the rest of his days, working the cattle drives and spring roundups.

Criticizing the cattle barons for clinging to the past was all good and fine. But cowboys like himself had to accept the new reality. The glory days of the Longhorns was done. And Ty and Ella didn't need him underfoot.

And now the future was all light and brightness. Yes siree, helping Kitty establish a polo pony ranch would be a mighty fine adventure.

Then Kitty slipped into the room and his heart about stopped.

The horsey woman in top hat and riding breeches was nowhere to be seen.

Uncertainty shone in her lovely eyes. She spun in a circle, so her gauzy white nightgown twisted around her lithe body and her thick brown hair swayed over her back. She bit her lip. "What do you think?"

His gut tightened. He swallowed. "Kitty-Girl, I'm going to die of starvation over here if you don't hurry up and kiss me."

A beautiful smile lit her face and she rushed into his arms. "Kiss me, Wy. And don't stop until we are true husband and wife."

Wyatt tasted of her kisses. "Are you always this bossy?"

She smiled against his mouth. "Do you want to waste time talking?"

Challenge accepted, he kissed her with all the love and passion in his heart.

Yep, marriage to Kitty was going to bring a lifetime of surprises, adventure, and happiness.

Epilogue

Three Months Later

The summer sky stretched for miles over the newly christened Ponderosa Polo Pony Ranch. Kitty hoped she never stopped marveling over the majesty of the Bighorn Mountains' jagged peaks, the swaths of green pastureland, and the towering pines that had inspired the name of the ranch.

She cherished the daily rides she and Wyatt took, exploring the boundaries of their vast property, searching out the various niches holding streams, waterfalls, and rugged buttes.

Wyatt would tease, saying they looked like a Wild West sideshow, with her in her top hat and matching silk-trimmed riding habit, and sitting an English saddle, and him outfitted in his white Stetson and fringed buckskin jacket, and sitting a western saddle.

And he loved it when she replied in an exaggerated British accent, assuring him that breeding quick, agile polo ponies with strong, surefooted Quarter Horses was jolly good and would produce champion offspring.

They were melding their lives together quite nicely. They had joined Henrietta and Theodore's polo club. And she and Wyatt had decided to establish a Hereford breeding operation, as well as the polo-pony program.

They had both been tremendously pleased when Mother and Mr. Wilcox approached them about purchasing his ranch. One of many cattle barons cutting their losses and pulling up stakes, Mr. Wilcox was happy traveling through Europe with Mother on an extended honeymoon.

Their Ponderosa Polo Pony Ranch sat adjacent to Sweet Creek Ranch, affording many visits and family gatherings. Freckled-face Billy could not have been prouder or more pleased when Kitty and Wyatt offered him the job of ranch foreman. Though only fifteen, he like many boys in the West grew up quickly. That was especially so of the second-chance boys.

Young Billy far exceeded Milton in the areas of maturity and trustworthiness. But she held more hope for her brother than when they had first arrived in America.

Accepting her and Wyatt's conditions and offer, Milton had stayed with them for two months before setting out for New York City to throw his hat into the stock exchange ring.

Her brother had gained weight, and his color had improved. He appeared to have found a measure of peace and purpose by overseeing the return of the stolen snuffbox and placing advertisements in the London and Somerset newspapers and by confessing his guilt and making proper apologies. He hired a new manager to see to the rebuilding of the estate.

Would the transformation last? She could not say. But she hoped Milton would find lasting peace and enjoy a happy life.

Upon his departure, he surprised her by hugging her and shedding a few tears and saying he would miss her. And she cried when he thanked her for not hating him for wronging her in such abominable fashion.

They shared a teary laugh when she pointed out that minus Milton's trickery and disgraceful behavior, she would never have met and married Wyatt.

Milton and Wyatt had reminded her that minus her bravery, none of what followed would have been possible.

 Cresting the sweeping rise overlooking the three-story, castle-like pine lodge at the heart of the Ponderosa Ranch, she drew Lady Winsome to a stop to admire the new polo field and view the progress of the construction of the steepled stable.

Wyatt dashed up on Charger. "What has you looking so happy, Kitty-Girl?"

Her ponies used to be her only joy. But Wyatt's love had become as essential to her as air. "I was thinking about all the amazing stories we will have to tell our children."

Wyatt graced her with a beautiful smile. "*The cattle rustler and his runaway bride*. Hoo wee, that will be a wild tale."

Father had said, *"Do not need anyone."*

But she no longer lived by that rule.

Kitty knew the precious gifts that were hers.

The ponies. Ponderosa Polo Pony Ranch.

The comfort of family. True happiness and love.

Wyatt.

And she would cherish each with her whole heart, always.

Author Note

Thank you for reading *The Cattle Rustler and the Runaway Bride*! If you are so inclined, I'd love a review of *The Cattle Ruster and the Runaway Bride*. Reviews can be hard to come by. You, the reader, have the power to make or break a book.

For more information about my books please visit:

WandaAnnThomas.com

For the latest news, cover reveals, and more sign up for my newsletter.

mad.ly/signups/117768/join

All the best,
Wanda Ann Thomas

Series Titles

~ **Brides of Sweet Creek Ranch** ~
(Sweet Historical Westerns)

Made in the USA
Lexington, KY
05 January 2019